With Her Body

Conversation Pieces

A Small Paperback Series from Aqueduct Press

Subscriptions available: www.aqueductpress.com

Fall 2004

1. The Grand Conversation
   Essays by L. Timmel Duchamp
2. With Her Body
   Short Fiction by Nicola Griffith
3. Changeling
   Novella by Nancy Jane Moore

Spring 2005

4. Counting on Wildflowers
   An Entanglement by Kim Antieau
5. The Traveling Tide
   Short Fiction by Rosaleen Love
6. The Adventures of the Faithful Counselor
   A Narrative Poem by Anne Sheldon
7. Ordinary People
   A Collection by Eleanor Arnason

About the Aqueduct Press Conversation Pieces Series

The feminist engaged with sf is passionately interested in challenging the way things are, passionately determined to understand how everything works. It is my constant sense of our feminist-sf present as a grand conversation that enables me to trace its existence into the past and from there see its trajectory extending into our future. A genealogy for feminist sf would not constitute a chart depicting direct lineages but would offer us an ever-shifting, fluid mosaic, the individual tiles of which we will probably only ever partially access. What could be more in the spirit of feminist sf than to conceptualize a genealogy that explicitly manifests our own communities across not only space but also time?

Aqueduct's small paperback series, Conversation Pieces, aims to both document and facilitate the "grand conversation." The Conversation Pieces series presents a wide variety of texts, including short fiction (which may not always be sf and may not necessarily even be feminist), essays, speeches, manifestoes, poetry, interviews, correspondence, and group discussions. Many of the texts are reprinted material, but some are new. The grand conversation reaches at least as far back as Mary Shelley and extends, in our speculations and visions, into the continually-created future. In Jonathan Goldberg's words, "To look forward to the history that will be, one must look at and retell the history that has been told." And that is what Conversation Pieces is all about.

L. Timmel Duchamp

Jonathan Goldberg, "The History That Will Be" in Louise Fradenburg and Carla Freccero, eds., *Premodern Sexualities* (New York and London: Routledge, 1996)

Published by Aqueduct Press
PO Box 95787
Seattle, WA 98145-2787
www.aqueductpress.com

09 08 07 06 05 04   1 2 3 4 5

ISBN: 0-9746559-4-5

Library of Congress Cataloging-in-Publication Data
Griffith, Nicola
With Her Body/Nicola Griffith.–1st ed.
p. cm.
1. Science Fiction. 2. Lesbian Fiction. 3. Feminist Fiction
I. Title

Cover Design by Lynne Jensen Lampe
Book Design by Kathryn Wilham
Original Block Print of Mary Shelley by Justin Kempton: www.writersmugs.com

Cover photo of Pleiades Star Cluster
NASA Hubble Telescope Images
STScI-2004-20
http://hubble.nasa.gov/image-gallery/astronomy-images.html
Credit: NASA, ESA, and AURA/Caltech

Printed in the USA

Conversation Pieces
Volume 2

With Her Body

Short Fiction

by

Nicola Griffith

with an Afterword by

L. Timmel Duchamp

Contents

❧ *Touching Fire*

That summer I was working nights at Talulah's to pay the rent until school opened again in the fall. It was Wednesday night, getting on time to close, and there was one woman left, nursing a beer over in the corner under the bass speaker. She was small, asian-dark, her dusty black hair cut in spikes, and not an ounce of fat on her, but not frail, definitely not frail.

I had to ask her to move her feet so I could get the mop under the table.

"My name's Nadia," she said, "and I'm a National Treasure."

"Right," I said, because the customer always is.

She moved her legs, anyhow. And finished off her beer. Then she looked around like she hadn't seen the place before. It was hard to tell what she thought of it. Talulah's is better than some places, worse than others. I've seen plenty of women's bars, though, and I like this one. On nights when I'm here as a paying customer and the women are high-stepping, flashing lean muscle and white teeth, and the floor almost moves with the weight of the music, it's a fine place, a place of possibility and excitement. But now, with the music down low, and the people paired off and gone, the harsh overhead light showed puddles of spilled beer on the floor and stains on the wall.

"Thursdays are the best," I offered, leaning on my mop. "And of course, I'll be here then." I gave her my best smile.

That's when she pushed back her chair and looked at me. Her eyes were very dark brown. Black maybe. "How do you do that?"

"What?"

"Trust a stranger. You shouldn't."

"It's never done me any harm."

Her smile was strange, twisty and self-mocking. "I do believe you mean that. You trust me." She said it slowly, like she was tasting the words. Then she nodded once, sharply. "Trust for trust then. But when the time comes, just make sure my guards don't see you talking to me."

Drugs, I thought, but she didn't look like she used. Too healthy. "Guards?"

"Privacy isn't one of the privileges of a National Treasure."

Then she slid out of her chair like she was made of oiled snake, not woman, and left.

That night I lay awake in my efficiency, thinking of the way she moved, of her black eyes, of her voice skating through several layers at once, like ocean currents.

Thursday, she was back. She was wearing black, the same dusty charcoal black as her hair. It made her skin look warm and rich, like cello wood. I slipped out from behind the bar and took a couple of beers to her table.

"You didn't get my name last time," I said, and put a beer in front of her. "I'm Kate." I held out my hand. She turned away, pretending she hadn't seen it.

"Go," she said, not looking at me. "My guards are here."

"Oh?" I glanced around, casually. "Where?" Sometimes if you humor people, they quit.

Not Nadia.

"Over by the pool table. Two of them. Earrings, short hair. One has beer, the other a shot glass." She'd just described the entire clientele. But she wasn't finished. "They're both wearing loose jackets. They have guns."

If she didn't want me at her table she just had to say so. But the thing was, I think she did want me there. I stayed.

She watched the dance floor for a minute. "Meet me in the bathroom in five minutes," then she got up to play the pinball machine.

I served a couple of people and kept watch on the two women by the pool table. Their faces were in shadow, but one had an outwardly bent little finger, like it had been broken and badly set. They didn't even glance at Nadia.

In the bathroom, Nadia was by the mirror, standing with feet wide and balanced, hands relaxed, but I could tell she was humming with tension. Even in the harsh neon, she was beautiful.

"I don't know why I'm doing this," she said.

I didn't, either.

She spread lean hands, as though offering something. "My name is Nadia Amin. I'm a National Treasure because I'm a LAOM dancer. The only one. I'm here in Atlanta because I'm helping Kyoto-TEC with their latest ad campaign. And when I'm not filming the commercials I'm working with a research team to figure out why I'm the only one who can do it."

"Do what?"

"The dance." She was impatient, but I didn't understand a word.

"Look," I said, "I'm a communication systems major. I don't know anything about larm dancing. Is that like ballet?"

Her hands curled, like claws. "L-A-O-M," she said, "Light Activated Orchestral Machines. I dance them." She must have seen my bewilderment. "They work by laser. I arrange them on a stage, dance through the beams of light, activating them to make music."

That sounded interesting. "Like those musician robot computers from Taiwan?"

"No. These are actual musical instruments. They're not pre-programmed."

I'd worked with light before, semester before last. It's tricky stuff. Every flicker of movement alters the parameters. "That's impossible."

Her smile was a slow slide of lips back from teeth. "Not for me. But as I said, I'm the only one."

That smile made me nervous. "You said you were a National Treasure. I didn't know they could apply that to people."

"They couldn't. Until now. I was a, ah, guest of the state, but Kyoto-TEC got wind of what I could do and hired some very good lawyers. They argued I was unique, and valuable, a national resource to whom normal rules should not apply." Again, that slow slide of lips. "Maybe they bribed the judge. Anyway, she agreed to bind me over to Kyoto-TEC. So here I am."

"Yes," I said, not knowing where that was, exactly.

"They've got a lot of money invested in me. And I'm unique. They do everything for me, give me anything I ask for."

She had no responsibilities. Like a child. I couldn't really imagine how it might be to live like that. "Is that what the guards are for, then? To make sure you stay safe?"

Her laugh clattered around the cold shiny spaces of the bathroom like a thrown knife, and I remembered she was a dancer, and dancers are very strong. She took hold of my arm. "You really shouldn't trust me," she said softly, then walked out into the dark and slam of the bar.

I stayed to wash my face and try to understand what the hell was going on.

When I got back out, she was gone. So were the two women by the pool table.

My apartment is five flights up. At night, when I'm tired, they're hell to climb, and I swear I'll look for a first floor apartment in the morning. But in the mornings I always relent: I'd taken the room because of the view. There's nothing like watching dawn come up over Piedmont Park, turning the trees to peach and orange and gold. Not that I'm often awake at that time.

Monday morning I was: Nadia was sitting at the end of my bed. She held out a DVD, between two fingers.

"I thought you might like to watch me dance."

"Christ…" I levered myself onto my elbow. She was still there; it was still dawn.

She smiled. "You look very soft when you're asleep. Very vulnerable."

She was wearing midnight blue, and her lips looked like plums. I waited, fascinated by those lips, too confused to ask questions. She leaned forward, slowly. I couldn't take my eyes off her mouth. She laid the disk on my chest. I clutched it to me, still stupid with sleep. "I don't have a player."

Nadia turned, looked around the bare white walls. She'd probably spent more money getting her hair cut than I had furnishing the whole efficiency. "No TV either."

"Where are your bodyguards, anyway."

"Everywhere." She stood up, sleepy lidded, like a cat, rocking my bed, sending my hormone count sky-high. She leaned over me again and tapped the disk I was still clutching to my chest. "I'll leave that for you."

She slung me a smile over her shoulder as she opened the door and stepped through. The locks clicked shut behind her.

It was only then that I wondered how she'd known where to find me, and how the hell she'd gotten in. *You really shouldn't trust me….*

Two and a half hours later the super banged on my door. "Package for you downstairs."

"I'll get it later."

"Came by special delivery. You gotta sign for it. Guys are waiting."

He sounded like one of those phone sex ads: Call Now, Guys Are Waiting. How could I resist? "I'm coming."

It was an HDTV flat panel, with DVD player and surround-sound home theatre system.

"I can't pay for this!" I said to the three men in overalls.

"Shipping bill says 'pre-paid,' lady. You want it or not?"

It was a Kyoto-TEC shipping bill. Nadia. But how had she done it so fast? And why? I thought about her crazy laugh, and bodyguards with guns.

"Lady…" They were getting impatient.

I nodded. "Follow me."

The screen went from black to white letterbox: an unmoving shot of a white-walled room with bare boards polished by age and countless generations of dancing feet. What looked like seven unfinished metal barrels, each a different girth and height, squatted on the floor in a huge irregular circle. Thick cables ran back from each and disappeared off screen. Nadia was tinkering with the insides of the leftmost barrel; she straightened abruptly, flicked a switch. A red eye glowed on the closed panel. She moved to the next one. The camera remained fixed on the center of the circle. The red light glowed on the second barrel. She went to the third.

A neat line of print appeared in the lower right corner of the screen: *Day two: initial assessment performance with Kyoto-TEC prototype LAOMs.*

I could tell by the way she walked that her muscles would feel tight under her skin, coiled, ready. Pre-performance nerves.

By now, red glowed on six of the seven barrels. Nadia leaned, flicked the switch on the last one and stepped to the middle of the circle. Her feet were bare. She wore the same dusty black as the second time she'd come to Talulah's, and no jewelry. Her hair was longer than I was used to seeing it, and she looked tired and tense: maybe it was she who was being assessed, not the machines.

She raised her arms. The light in the studio dimmed, and each of the seven barrels suddenly splayed dozens, hundreds of ribbons of light up and out, like straight-line fountain water. At first it looked like white light, but it wasn't, not quite. One barrel poured with ivory, another with sepia; a third shimmered like a heat haze over sand.

Nadia stayed immobile, in the exact center of the ring, black clothes untouched by light. She was smiling faintly, her skin sheened with sweat, her breathing even; not nervous now, just ready.

I'd never seen anyone move like Nadia did. One moment she was standing like she'd been carved from wood a hundred years dead, the next she leapt away in a twirling half-turn, slashing her arms down through several beams of different colored light, flick flick flick, faster than I could follow, making music. Every time her hair, or a fingertip or a crease of her clothes, the heel of her left foot or the thrust of a hip went through light, there was a sound. Nadia kept moving, and the music poured from the barrels: tubular bells and violas, french horns and African drums: sampled music, like a light-operated Fairlight Series IV. Only instead of taking sampled and digitally stored music that had already been programmed into coherent sequences and then manipulating the waveform using a light pen, she was doing it all simultaneously, with her body, using dance to make music. It was like watching a shuttle liftoff: impossible, but happening right before your eyes.

It was fast music, sun-on-dragonfly music; music like the thousand and one flowers nodding in a field and the flyers and burrowers that played above and below. Light-hearted music, but complex, with the rhythms of life and death: computer-aided Grieg, or Camel with violins; marvellous music, intoxicating. And creating it, spinning in it, sweat flying from her skin and making its own, little music, was Nadia: charcoal tunic and trousers stained black in patches, hair slicked down to her scalp and half-smile gone, replaced by utter concentration. I could see and hear the work: muscles bunched and stretched, bare feet thumped on boards, breath whistled. For a few seconds—half a minute—she hit her groove, and the dancing and music came together in a perfect, pattern. Her sheened arms slid and swam through the light like fish, faster, faster, and the bass and treble, the horns and strings and woodwinds all fit together in an intricate jigsaw making me laugh out loud at the wonder of it. But then she put a foot too far forward and the cello faltered, and the synergy of movement and sound was lost. Once again, it was just a woman dancing beautifully, making marvellous music.

The screen blanked, cutting picture and sound mid-bar.

I blinked, took a shaky breath. So that was LAOM dancing. I picked up the remote, wanting to watch it all again, in slow motion, but the screen flicked back to white. More?

This time the lettering came up first: *Day 163, Performance, Mark III Kyoto-TEC LAOMs.* Five or six months later, then. And this time they had a real camera operator on the job: a pan shot of the LAOMs first, eight of them now, seven arranged in a squashed-looking circle, the eighth off-center. They weren't the crude things of *Day 2*, either: these were beautifully finished machines, wooden cases gleaming, plates made of burnished high-tensile alloys.

Nadia stood, ready: not the tired, tense woman-under-trial of *Day 2*, but a different Nadia.

She was wearing arterial red; there were long feathers hanging from one ear, and the fingers of both hands were tipped with razorblade extensions of dull gray metal. Around her right ankle was a thick ring with a spike on the outside. The quality of her waiting was different, too: not an absence, but a presence. She brooded, like a caged animal, like a storm building on the horizon: a creature of brass and blood. I expected her to slide back her lips from red teeth and hiss.

The LAOMs suddenly spread their fingers of light—jungle colors this time, purples and golds and turquoise—like exotic pineapples sprouting spikes of virulent greenery. Nadia moved her head, letting the feather in her left ear swing out and touch a turquoise ribbon: a parrot cawed. She moved her head again; the parrot screamed over the thumping start of a deep heartbeat. The camera pulled back its focus: Nadia's foot was tapping deliberately, the spike cutting back and forth through a low gold stream of light. Then she turned, fast as a panther stalking, and the music came pouring forth.

It was murder music, heat-and-sex music, and Nadia was leaping, whirling, sliding and tricking her way through those thousands of frozen Roman-candle lights. She never once missed the heartbeat. Wherever she was, at whatever speed, that footspike came down dead on the beat, every time, over and over.

I could hardly breathe.

She reached and sliced through hot ruby and hummingbird blue with her metal-tipped fingers, and the ribbons of light from two LAOMs began to rotate. She moved faster and faster, but, paradoxically, everything seemed to slow down, become perfectly defined. Each note, each layer of music was absolutely separate from the rest; each beat seemed to have all the time in the world to swell and crest and ebb, then swell and sound again. My heart was thumping and I wanted to shout, or scream, or die. I felt on the edge of something profound.

And the sound and the dance built, and Nadia's ankle spike never missed a beat, only now she was using her fingertips and her feathers and the flick and swirl of her diaphanous trousers to create counter-beats, and rhythm upon rhythm upon rhythm.

It was only when the screen blanked again, releasing me, that I found I was crushing the remote in my hands, bruising my palms; that I was able to cry. I sat on the couch for fifteen or twenty minutes, coughing up sobs from deep places I never even knew I had. Nadia had ripped something away, torn aside the veil we normally wear every day to survive in the city. She made me smell life, feel it, touch it, taste it. She made me want…something. Something more, much more than I had now. She had made me see that there was more to life than just existing the best I could day by day. Life was to be lived; to be taken and shaken and sucked dry, used up. Every moment was precious. I wanted to reach out and touch her fire, bathe in it, be clothed by it.

Life. Nadia made me ache for it, fiercely, from my bones out. But inside I was scared, as well as excited: there was never adventure without risk.

Monday and Tuesday nights Talulah's stays closed, so they're my lazy days, my weekend. I spent the rest of Monday doing errands: stocking up on food, doing my laundry, the usual stuff. Every so often, vacuum cleaner going, or plate halfway to the sink, I'd pause and look over at the huge entertainment center that took up more space than my kitchenette, and wonder: Why? And that, of course, was closely followed by: How? How had Nadia found out where I lived? She didn't even know my last name—at least, I hadn't told her. And how had she managed to get everything here so fast? And that all led back to why. Why was she doing this?

You really shouldn't trust me.

And then, of course, I'd have to put the plate down or turn off the vacuum cleaner, and play the disk again, just to reassure myself that I'd seen what I'd seen.

I slept badly that night, and my sleep was full of erotic dreams of a feral and primordial Nadia, a Nadia without inhibition.

I woke up Tuesday almost as tired as when I'd gone to sleep, and with my body giving me unmistakable signals that now it knew *exactly* what it yearned after. I sighed. I had to do something about this.

My laptop was ancient, a hand-me-down from Mom, with dysfunctional battery backup and zero compatibility with any known modem. So I stuck a disk in my pocket and took the MARTA train downtown to the main Fulton County reference library.

I read first about research trends in computer-assisted composition. Nothing unexpected there: lots of gabble about Fairlights and court cases pertaining to digital sampling and copyright, and one tiny article in an obscure journal about the possibilities of adapting computers so that physically challenged people could use light to compose music. There was a counter-article detailing why such light-parametered composition computers would, in practice, be impossible to use. I checked the author of the first article and found he worked at Columbia, in the music and computer labs sponsored by Kyoto-TEC. Ah hah. The article was dated two years ago. Nothing since then. Just as Nadia said: new stuff, and the prevailing opinion was that it simply couldn't be done. But Kyoto-TEC had watched the work done in their laboratory and decided differently.

Next, I looked up National Treasure provisions and precedent-setting court cases. There it was, under *Decisions: Kyoto-TEC v. US Govt.*, and the date was about right, seven months ago. Jackpot. I downloaded the abstract.

I ran a search for *Amin, Nadia + interview* and found two articles that were relevant. The first was nothing much, just a paragraph in the *Seattle Times* about three students graduating with double honors at the University of Washington. Nadia was one of them, majoring in dance and music theory. The second was more interesting.

It was dated eight months after the first—and ten after the piece I'd read earlier on the Kyoto-TEC lab researcher's theories. According to the paper, Nadia Amin, a promising young student enrolled at the Seattle Academy of Performing Arts, had blown the entire electrical system of the Gardner Annex while trying to perform something she called "Zeus and Semele: An Exercise in Light Composition."

I looked at the color image of the gutted annex for a long time. Now I knew that it was at least possible for Nadia to be who she said she was. I was looking forward to getting home and reading the abstract of the court case, to finding out just what it took to be declared a National Treasure as opposed to a National Menace.

When I got home there was a message on my machine from my mother, reminding me that today was my father's birthday and I was supposed to be going over for dinner with the rest of the family. I'd forgotten of course. I dropped the disks on my couch and sprinted for the shower. The abstract would have to wait.

On Wednesday I woke up well after midday to the hot, still air of a coming storm. My skin felt tight and I had a headache; the room was stifling. I decided to risk over-loading the ancient electrical circuits and turned on my window air conditioner to cool the room.

I always find it hard to concentrate before a storm.

After I'd spent an unnecessary hour puttering about with breakfast and watching local news on my HDTV, I finally got dressed and settled down with my laptop and the abstract of the court case.

I couldn't understand the first two pages, gobbledy-gook, all of it: lists of obscure statutes and indictment codes, and lots of *wheras*es and *hereinafter*s. The air condi-tioner was laboring, making my head thump. I frowned and concentrated, and around page five the words began to make sense.

The judge, one Honorable Harriet Thurman, agreed to admit the testimony of expert witness Dr. Schubert Macillvaney, psychiatrist. Macillvaney assured the court that Nadia Amin was not dangerous, except in certain already described circumstances, and that in his opin-ion there would be no danger to the public should she be released into the custody of Kyoto-TEC, as long as stringent prec—

The AC coughed once, horribly, and the current in my apartment died. The words on my screen blipped out.

I sat in the suddenly dark room and stared at my blank screen. *Released into the custody*… What had Nadia done? Blown up another academy?

You really shouldn't trust me. I thought of her shiny laugh-ter that night at Talulah's; her talk of bodyguards and guns; how she had found me, found my apartment, bypassed the locks, sat on my bed. But I also remembered the way she had leaned forward, so close; the way she moved, oh god the way she moved.…

Finally, the level of darkness in the apartment got through to me: it wasn't just the gathering storm, it was getting late. I scribbled a note for the Super about my burned out fuses and left for work.

Talulah gave me some hard looks; I rang up the wrong money several times and twice kept customers waiting while I stared off into space, thinking of Nadia with her ankle spike and metal fingernails, the way she curved and arched, her blood red lips....

The women were restless tonight, and Jenny the DJ played strange, hard music with a driving slow beat. The air shimmered with tension and heat. We sold more shots of tequila and vodka that night than any other Wednesday since the fourth of July three years ago. I got bought a few, too, and drank them down eagerly, as though the clear liquid might give me some answers.

Nadia came in a little after midnight. I'd been waiting for her of course. She was wearing diaphanous dark red pants and shirt through which showed her dancer's shadowed curves. I could almost feel those strong muscles under my hands, and wondered whether if I ran my fingers down her silky calves I'd find a metal spike around her ankle. I turned away as she took a table near the dance floor and served two women who had just come in. They ordered beer. When the taller one reached out to pay, I noticed her little finger was bent. They both wore jackets, even though it was hot. I swallowed, gave them change. They nodded and took stools at the bar. Where they could watch Nadia.

"Think I'll go round up the empties, see if I can scare up some more orders," I said to Talulah. She gave me another of those hard looks, but nodded.

I hit four tables before Nadia's, trotted back and forth with more shot glasses of vodka and tequila. When I thought the bodyguards weren't looking, I cruised up behind Nadia.

"A drink, ma'am?"

She looked up with those sleepy-lidded eyes, those dangerous, gorgeous eyes. She smiled, and I knew she knew I'd watched her dance. She could probably smell it on me. "A drink, yes." Her eyes flicked to the jacketed women at the bar and back. I nodded that I'd noticed them. "Bring me a surprise," she said, and turned away.

I took her a shot glass of Prairie Fire: tequila with seven drops of tabasco sauce. She swallowed it down without looking at me. "Bring me another." I brought her another. She watched the women on the dance floor moving belly to back and drank it down as fast as the first. "Now you can watch me dance."

She stood up, still without looking at me, and walked onto the floor, moving through the heaving crowd with an easy reach-the-rhythm step that wasn't either syncopated or bang on the beat like a march. Then she danced.

At first she seemed to be more or less standing still, but her hips were moving, slowly, and she began to run her hands up and down the air before her. Now and again she moved a leg slightly, bending out at the knee, easily, to the music. Then her hands moved, one down, one stroking the air between throat and belly level, up and down. She looked at me then, and smiled, and I blushed a hot, deep red.

Here, she was saying, *this is what I'll do to you when I take you to bed.*

I couldn't bear it, I wanted her so much, but I couldn't turn away: I stood there, trembling, helpless.

The music changed, and a woman with long hair started dancing at Nadia, who laughed and danced back, ignoring me. I wanted to kill that woman with long hair. I pushed my way through the crowds and out an emergency side door exit into the parking lot.

The night tasted of cars driven too fast and braked too hard, of beer and fragile laughter, of one o'clock in the morning. The sky was dark and thick with thunderclouds. There was a flash in the west, and a low rumble. Sultry, restless weather.

Music blared loud and was cut off again as someone stepped out into the night. I didn't turn, but tilted my head back to watch the stormcloud bunching and heaving like overheated muscle.

A hand touched the back of my neck. Nadia. The hand slid around to stroke my throat. "Let's go," she said in my ear, and, god help me, I went, just like that, without telling Talulah, without even *thinking* of telling Talulah, without thinking of the court case or Nadia's admonitions not to trust her. I walked to my car, her hand still on my neck, without saying a word, without thinking at all.

The rain started on the way back to my apartment, fat ripe drops. I wanted to drive fast, but Nadia laid a hand on my thigh and I kept the speedometer exactly at thirty. No dark sedan followed us. My blood felt like molten metal.

At the apartment building, we still didn't speak. Our breathing matched, heavy and rhythmic, as we climbed the five flights of stairs. When we reached the top, Nadia stroked the back of my neck with one hand and tapped in my lock code with the other. We went in.

The power was still off, but the bed sheets shone sodium yellow in the glow of streetlights reflected from rain-wet streets. Nadia watched, unspeaking, her face in shadow, as I undressed. I felt as though I was stripping off my history, my inhibitions, my safety. This was right here, right now, like playing with fulminate of mercury. I didn't know what to expect. All I knew was that I wanted her to run a fingertip through the sweat in the small of my back, I wanted her to hold me with those strong arms and iron legs, I wanted her breath hot on my face as her lips came closer. I wanted her, wanted her, wanted her.

Hours later, Nadia stood naked by the open window, watching the night. I lay across the bed, fascinated by her, drunk with her, surfeited, stuffed tight as a drum with sweat and sex and the memory of skin between gentle teeth, of strong fingers, and her belly on my back and arm around my hips.

When the storm had been over the roof over Nadia over me over the bed, the rain had been so heavy it had leaked through the old roof tiles, seeping down inside the walls, mixing with the plaster made of red Georgia clay, making the whitewashed walls weep blood.

That had been hours ago. The storm was gone now, and all that remained of the rain were dripping gutters and the glisten on the treetops in Piedmont Park. The streets were quiet; it was not long before dawn.

"At this time of night," she said, "I can almost believe it would be possible to fall out of a high window and be buoyed up by the darkness itself, that we could fly." She turned back to look at me, and the breath caught in my throat. "Do you believe in flying?"

Yes. But I couldn't speak. She had made me fly for hours; I had soared. I couldn't see her face, but I knew she smiled. She moved a step towards the bed, and though the streetlights reflected from below turned her eye the mad marigold of a hawk's, and I was scared, my blood roared hot under my skin, and the tendons running inside my thighs tightened in anticipation. She laughed, a low, double-cream laugh. "Perhaps you would like me to come a little closer?"

I woke up the next day, alone. The window was closed. I sat up. Had I dreamed it? But the walls were streaked with plaster blood, the sheets were torn, and the room smelled of her, my hands and my hair and belly smelled of her. I laughed out loud: pleased with myself; a little ashamed; exhausted.

There was a yellow sticky note on the TV screen: *Three o'clock, in the park.*

A typically Nadia note. No *Please* or *Thank you* or *Can you make it?*

The power was still off and I was showering in the dark when someone knocked on the door. I didn't much feel like getting out all wet, so I ignored the tapping and turned the spray up to full force. If they knocked again, I wouldn't hear it.

I soaped myself absently, shivering as I remembered Nadia's hands, the way she had touched the back of my neck and said, "Let's go."

How was I going to persuade Talulah to let me keep my job? I couldn't believe I'd just walked out like that, without telling her.

I sighed and rinsed off, pulled a towel off the rack. I needed that job. Perhaps Talulah would believe a sudden case of ptomaine poisoning, a night in the emergency room.... I padded through into the main room, toweling myself dry.

There was a woman staring at the stained wall.

Obviously she had just let herself in: the door was still swinging closed. She spun around when she heard me. Crooked Finger.

"Oh," she said, looking at me, then the wall. "Then it's not...." She shut up, but not before I heard the relief in her voice.

I stood there, naked and confused. "What's not what?"

She sidled toward the door.

"Wait," I said. Some of my shock was wearing off, but not the confusion. "What are you doing here?" She opened the door. I noticed the gloves. "Wait just a god-damned minute—"

She bolted through the door, slammed it shut behind her.

I stared at it blankly, then leaped after her. "You stop right there!" But she was disappearing down the third flight of stairs. I swore and started after her. Old Mr. Hinklemeier popped his head out of his door, and his eyes bugged. I was still naked.

Damn everything to hell and back.

Nadia was by the lake, feeding the ducks. I watched her for a while from the trees. She threw bread like she did everything else: with utter concentration, a kind of ferocity that did not allow for interruption. The ducks didn't care. They swam around and around, performing for their supper.

I stepped out of the trees, enjoyed the way her pupils blazed big for a moment when she saw me. *Mine*, I thought with that absurd proprietorship of the day-after, and smiled.

She smiled back, and the day suddenly seemed brighter, cleaner. "Watch this," she said, and threw a single big piece of bread into the center of the swimming ducks. One of the smaller ones, a mallard with a green head and flashing eye, thrust its way through the squabbling covey and snatched the bread. "He does that every time." She sounded admiring.

"Why not just throw smaller pieces, so they can all have some?"

"I like to watch them fight."

She gave me some bread, and we threw it in companionable silence for a few minutes. I did my best to make sure all the ducks got some.

We walked slowly around the water. Two men followed us at a discreet distance. "Are they watching us?"

Nadia did not even look over to see who I meant. "Someone's always watching me."

"They weren't at Talulah's, that first time." Or last night, in my apartment.

"That was special. It was my birthday," and she stooped to pick up a stone which she tossed into the water.

She had been all alone that night, just her and five empty beer glasses and the end of an evening. Her birthday. I wanted to gather her up in my arms, but she was standing so straight and staring out over the water with such concentration that I didn't.

"There was one in my apartment, earlier. One of the women that came into Talulah's last night." She didn't turn, but a shift in her shoulders told me she was very interested. "She must have thought there was no one home. I'd just come out of the shower, stark naked, and we stared at each other. I don't know who was more surprised, her or me."

Now Nadia was looking at me. I could see the pleats in her brown-black eyes, pleats I had noticed for the first time last night when she had been moving over me, running her....

"Did she say anything?"

"Um? Oh, no, not really. Just looked at me, looked at the wall, and bolted."

I hadn't realized Nadia had been tense until her muscles relaxed and she turned back to look over the water, relieved.

"Nadia, what's going on? I don't understand any of this. First of all, you tell me not to trust you. Then guards with guns follow us about the place." I took her hand, trying to get rid of the awful fear that was suddenly hauling itself up my spine, one vertebra at a time. "They should know by now that you're safe with me, that I'm not some corporate assassin. I mean, what are these guards afraid of? And what are you afraid of? I really don't get this." Crooked Finger hadn't seemed upset to see me. If anything, she'd been relieved. "I don't like it. I'm not used to people letting themselves into my apartment as and when they feel like it. Even you."

Nadia didn't say anything. I sighed, and tugged her over to a bench. We sat down.

"Talk to me about this." Silence. "At least tell me how you did it, how you knew where to find me in the first place. How you managed to get through my locks."

She tilted her head back, stretched. The sunshine turned her throat to gold. "I told you: they give me everything I want; I have access to more than you can possibly imagine. As for finding you, that was easy. Kyoto-TEC have unofficial tendrils in every pie. I accessed the local IRS database and found there was only one employee at Talulah's whose first initial was K. So getting your last name was simple. Then I scanned the phone company's information for your address. Easy."

Just accessed the IRS database. Easy. Right. "What about the lock?"

"It's made by Kyoto-TEC. I found out what model it was, then asked one of the designers to show me how to compromise it."

Just like that. I wondered if she had any moral scruples at all. Like a child, she could have something, so she took it, right or wrong. And like a child she refused responsibility for what she did.

Children are notoriously fickle.

"I'd like a number where I can get in touch with you."

"I can reach you easily enough."

"I know. But I'd like a number. Just in case."

Nadia looked at me. "You don't understand," she said finally. Damn right I didn't. "I'm at everyone's beck and call, all the time. They whistle and I have to jump. I wanted, want, to have someone who won't do that to me, where I'm in charge."

"It doesn't have to be either/or," I said, and took her hand again. "And you have rights. You could make them give you time for yourself, privacy, like you did on your birthday."

"That was different. They gave me the time because they were desperate: I wasn't able to work anymore." She took her hand away. "Have you ever seen a swan with a lead fishing weight around its neck, choking? That was me. I couldn't dance, I couldn't fly with them wrapped around my neck like that. So they let me have a night, one night."

"Two nights," I said, and kissed her hand. She said nothing. "No?"

"Depends how long it took them to find out who you are, where you live. What time they managed to track us down."

I imagined Crooked Finger and her colleague crouching by the door, listening to my abandonment, and felt naked and furious. I wanted to march over to the two men standing by the lake and bang their heads together. But underneath my anger was the nagging feeling that I was missing something, something important.

"So," she said, "I'd like you to trust me. It's important that someone does. Trust me enough not to ask for my number."

I understood the need for privacy. The thought of never having it was appalling. If it was that important to her....

I nodded. She smiled at me, then blinked that lazy-lidded blink that sent desire curling through my belly. "Let's go back to your apartment," she said.

"I'll see you tonight or tomorrow night," she said as she left, three hours later.

It took me thirty minutes to summon up the energy to climb off the bed, but then I hurried: I still had to persuade Talulah to let me keep my job, and it wouldn't do to be late.

Talulah didn't believe my story, but forgave me anyway. The evening passed slowly. Nadia didn't come.

I climbed my five flights slowly, half expecting to find her in my apartment when I got there. Hope springs eternal.

For the first time since I'd rented it a year ago, the apartment seemed bleak and empty. At least the power was back on. The laptop blinked at me. I hesitated, then turned it off. Nadia deserved her privacy.

I was tired, and hungry, but all the food in the refrigerator had spoiled. Tomorrow. I'd deal with everything tomorrow.

I touched the stain on the wall and climbed into bed. The sheets smelled of her.

The reporter turned away from the rain streaked window. "Zeus and Semele," he said, "and she'll burn you. At least with two women it won't be a case of Leda and the Swan." Then he turned into Nadia. "Trust me." She laughed and the laughter took shape, dark, with wings, and flew out of the window. "You see," she said earnestly, walking towards me, "it's not a question of whether you trust me, but whether or not I can trust myself." She came closer and closer and I began to panic, then suddenly she was choking: a rope with weights was wrapping around her neck, snakelike. "No!" she screamed, "not this time!" and then the one strangling was me, and Crooked Finger was coming through the door with a mop and bucket and a big plastic bag.

I had other dreams, but that was the one I remembered when I woke up at midday.

Zeus and Semele. Some Greek myth or other. Uneasy dream logic.

Last night, if anyone had asked me, I would have told them I trusted Nadia completely, believed everything she said. I'd even thought that I no longer needed to read the court abstract, that I didn't wish to absorb others' comments on a woman I was beginning to care for. But sometime in the night, while I dreamed, little inconsistencies had floated up from my subconscious, and now they sat in a clump, demanding attention.

It's not a question of whether you trust me, but whether or not I can trust myself.... What did I know about Nadia, really?

When I climbed out of bed I ignored the laptop and went straight back to the library.

All the way back on the train, hours later, I stared at the smeared window, not seeing the city or reflections of the hot, bad-tempered commuters homeward bound; seeing nothing but a mind's-eye picture of the library screen, with those damning, damning words.

> After hearing assurances that Kyoto-TEC were well placed to foster and develop Nadia Amin's natural talents, to the eventual benefit of all Americans, Judge Thurman indicated her willingness to transmute sentence and accord Amin status as National Treasure. The judge expressed some reservations

about Kyoto-TEC's precautions. K-T again called expert witness Macillvaney, psychiatrist, who reiterated that Amin was unlikely to prove dangerous to the general public. Despite this, he assured the court, K-T would—under his personal supervision—undertake to keep Amin under observation at all times, and to physically restrain her at those times of greatest risk—during solar and atmospheric storms.

K-T's counsel reminded Judge Thurman that the Secretary of Labor had asked for special consideration of this case, given the number of jobs likely to be at risk should K-T go into receivership, which it assuredly would if their investment in Amin was not realized.

Judge Thurman expressed further reservations but admitted that given the recent directives from the Supreme Court she had little choice. She reminded Kyoto-TEC that the untimely death of a young man at Amin's hands was a good reason, a very good reason, for the original sentence of life in a secure mental institution, and she reiterated her promise that if K-T ever forgot that, if they ever deviated by one iota from their proposed security arrangements, she would send them all to jail, Supreme Court or no Supreme Court.

Whereupon Justice Thurman formally declared Nadia Amin to be a National Treasure, thereby superseding state jurisdiction and overturning any earlier sentences handed down in the United States of America, and remanded Amin into the protective custody of Kyoto-TEC, incorporated, under the conditions set forth in Document 157-3B, until such time as a higher court declared said ruling null and void.

And then, because I hadn't wanted to think about what I'd just read, I'd looked up the story of Zeus and Semele.

I got to the bar early. I didn't know what else to do. I must have been in a daze, because even now I don't remember what Talulah said, or what I said, or anything about the first couple of hours. I moved through the evening on auto-pilot, saying hi to the customers, laughing at their jokes, making the right change.

When Nadia walked in the evening did not so much come into sharp focus as ripple and reform around her, like a cloak. Even knowing what I knew, understanding the risks she had taken, I couldn't set aside the flood of memory images that overlay her appearance as she walked to a table: Nadia dancing at me; her hand on my thigh as we drove; turning with that mad marigold eye and asking from the rainshadow, "Do you believe in flying?"

I had then.

Her keepers came in right on her heels. No more discreet distances; I guess that stain on the wall had really scared Crooked Finger. I walked around the bar, straight to Nadia's table.

She smiled. "I'll have another of those Prairie Fires."

I remembered the taste of tequila on her mouth. "Outside," I said. "Not the parking lot. The patio."

She raised her eyebrows, but got up and walked in front of me, outside. The air smelled of the honeysuckle Talulah had trained over the trellis.

She reached for me. My blood leaped like a wild thing and there was nothing more I wanted than to put myself under those hands, feel her cool, dry palms whispering over my skin, but I moved away.

She tilted her head, considered me. "Not tonight, Josephine?"

I almost changed my mind; she seemed so utterly normal, standing there with that puzzled look on her face. "I trusted you," I said.

She understood immediately: I knew. Her eyes were hooded. "The first time we met, I told you: never trust a stranger."

"You can't absolve yourself of responsibility like that, with words. I did trust you. And what of your words in the park? 'Trust me,' you said, 'trust me enough not to ask for my number.' Trust *you*! What about trusting me? Why didn't you tell me?"

"Because you wouldn't have loved me."

"You can't know that! You lied to me. You said the guards were there to protect you." *Is that why you have the guards?* I had asked. *To make sure you stay safe?* And she had laughed. At me. At my naïveté, my eagerness to believe what she told me. "But they weren't, were they? You have guards to protect people like me from you. That woman who came into my apartment was relieved because I was still alive: she thought the plaster stain on the wall was my blood. After all, you've already killed one person, they were going to put you away forever for it, so why not kill me too?"

"I would never kill you," she said quietly.

"I don't *know* that! How can I trust you when you've already lied to me so many times?"

"I never lied. You believed what you wanted."

"And you think that's not lying? That's a solipsism worthy of a child, not a grown woman! You knew what I believed, you knew it was untrue, that's pure deception."

"I would never hurt you," Nadia said again, and she sounded alone and vulnerable, and my heart almost broke.

"But you...I..." I just didn't know what to say. This woman had killed a man, and I still loved her. "Please, tell me what happened."

"I have a psychiatric condition that manifests itself in a confusion between sex and death. An active confusion. It's complicated by the fact that I also have a physiological condition, a brain imbalance that's affected by electrical storms."

"Don't. Don't quote at me. Tell me…" What? What was it I really wanted to know? That she wouldn't do it to me. That it was all a mistake. That she wasn't crazy. "Tell me what happened, and why."

"I threw him out of a window. In a storm. He didn't believe in flying." I couldn't tell what she was thinking. She seemed utterly alien. "You did."

"And if I hadn't?"

"You were in no danger. The guards were listening outside."

"No." I groped for words. "You gave them the slip. It was some sort of test. You were testing yourself. To see." She had deliberately put me in danger, had taken me to bed in a storm, when her poor mad brain could have made her do anything, when she knew she could not trust herself. Or…maybe she did. *Trust for trust, then,* she had said, that first night. I had trusted her; perhaps that had given her the ability to trust herself.

"You've made me feel so much." I couldn't describe it to her. She would never understand: she was different, elemental, a being clothed in fire.

…and, with child, the princess Semele asked her mysterious lover to reveal himself in his true nature and form. When Zeus refused, Semele denied him further access to her bed and body. In wrath, Zeus assumed the form of thunder and lightning, and Semele was consumed.…

But I wasn't some idiot peasant, six months pregnant, and Nadia was mortal. She bled, like I did, and felt, and needed. This wasn't impossible.

"Nadia—"

We looked at one another. She was lovely, lovely like a snake, like a twenty-one foot crocodile, like the edge of the world.

Music burst over us as Crooked Finger pushed open the door. We ignored her. Satisfied that we weren't feeling murderous, she withdrew.

I loved this woman. There had to be a way. "I think you should try therapy," I said, very fast, because I knew she wouldn't like the idea. "And there are drugs you could take, if you thought...when you maybe couldn't really trust yourself. Your trial was more than a year ago. There might be new treatments. Psychiatry is always changing, always moving on." She was shaking her head. "No. Don't make up your mind yet. Do you love me? No, forget I asked that. Don't say anything. I'm going to go back inside now, and serve more beer to more customers. I want you to leave. I want you to think about what I've said, and when you have an answer...when you have an answer..." My throat was closing up. "When you have an answer, let me know." I left her standing there, and stepped back into the smoke and heat of the bar.

When I got home, she was sitting in my bed. Streetlight turned her skin to gold and copper, and the shadows between her ribs were dark and mysterious as ancient bronze.

"Do you love me?" I asked from the doorway, without turning on the lights.

"I want you."

"That's not good enough," I said, but I was pulling off my clothes.

"Come here." She held me by the hips. "How shall I answer you? I'm crazy, not legally responsible for my actions." Her voice was hot and dark and rough as a cat's tongue. My nipples pebbled. "I'm the only one who can LAOM dance, because I'm crazy, crazy enough to believe I can fly, that I can do it." She kissed the place three inches above my navel, where all the nerves in the torso come together. "Everyone else knows it can't be done, so they don't do it." She kissed lower. "I'm mad enough to believe in myself, to believe that it can be done. Lie down." I did. "So I do it. Like an idiot savant. No one knows how I do it, but I do."

She lay down beside me and began rocking her palm on my belly. She spoke into my open mouth. "And you want me to go to some shrink and be cured of what it is that makes me believe I can fly, that makes me free. Open your legs." She started inside my knees and stroked my thighs gently, all the way up, cradled my buttocks in one hand. Her eyes were like holes. "I won't," she said.

Then she wrapped herself around me like a python.

I woke early, not long after dawn. She was sleeping on her stomach, head turned to the right, one leg bent at the knee, arms above her head, lips parted: perfect, right down to her eyelashes and fingernails and the downy hairs in the small of her back.

I won't, she had said. And she wouldn't.

With her eyes closed, I could forget that she'd killed someone, once. I was willing to take the chance. I wanted to rub her feet when they ached and listen while she complained about the weather; I wanted to see her laugh when I presented her with seventeen brightly-wrapped presents for her next birthday; I wanted to stand in line with her at Target to buy cheap shirts, and work out who owed what on the phone bill.

She sighed and turned her head to the left. Where she had been lying on it, her hair was flat and dark. I wanted to run my fingers through it. Instead, I slid quietly from the bed, pulled on some clothes and wrote a note to stick on the TV screen: *Gone shopping to make you a breakfast that'll put the nectar of the gods to shame.*

I took my time at the market. For the first time, I enjoyed sifting oatbran through my fingers, fascinated by its cream and gold flow, its smell of dust and biscuit. The rice flour was more gritty, and reminded me of almonds. While I waited for the orange honey to fold, heavy and slow, into my plastic tub, I imagined sitting outside in some Florida orchard with Nadia, listening to bees hum through the blossom.

I plumped each loaf of bread to find the freshest; picked up each piece of fruit individually, checking for that perfect, unblemished, ripe-to-bursting skin before I put it carefully in my basket. I even chose the eggs one by one.

I walked back through the early morning sunshine, then up the five flights of steps full of the marvel of the breakfast I would conjure from my paper sack: fruit salad, bran and banana muffins, eggs, toast....

The apartment door was open. The sticky note was gone. Nadia was gone. A strange woman was wiping down the light switches and door handles, and Crooked Finger was sitting on the edge of the bed, tapping something against her thigh. The DVD.

I put my sack down carefully on the kitchenette table. It needed a good scrub, I thought. I didn't ask what Crooked Finger and her colleague were doing, or where Nadia was.

"We'll have to take this, too," Crooked Finger said to me, meaning the disk. "I'm sorry."

"Are you?" I wasn't hostile, just tired. Very, very tired. She had the sense not to answer. I wondered how many times she had cleaned up after Nadia and whether she'd ever had to use a body bag.

The woman wiping things down gave a doorknob one last polish, nodded at us both, and left.

"She asked me to give you a message," Crooked Finger said.

I started taking out the eggs, one by one, and breaking them in a bowl. I rummaged for a fork, concentrated very hard on breaking the perfect golden hemispheres into stringy liquid.

"Here." She put a piece of paper by the bowl. A yellow sticky note. "I'm sorry," she said again. I just kept beating those eggs until the door clicked shut behind her.

I picked up the note.

Love can be a lead weight too, and I need to fly.

She had loved me, after all.

I'll never see her again; images don't count. And I somehow don't think there'll be many of those, despite Kyoto-TEC's high hopes. It's just a matter of time before, somewhere, with someone, Nadia loses control, and another body tumbles through the air on a rainy night; Crooked Finger and her fellow moppers-up won't always be able to fix the evidence. Then Nadia will go back to jail, or maybe she'll throw herself out of a window, try flying for real: she wouldn't be able to bear being shut up, never allowed to dance again.

I sold the entertainment center, painted out the stain on my wall; I bought new sheets and tucked the egg-stained sticky note in a drawer. But sometimes when I'm sweeping up at Talulah's, I imagine her sitting at that table, alone, like she was the first time, when I asked her to move her legs so I could mop the floor, and whenever the sky rumbles, or I'm driving through heavy rain, I feel a ghostly hand on my thigh, and smell tequila. I still burn for her fire.

Song of Bullfrogs, Cry of Geese

I sat by the side of the road in the afternoon sun and watched the cranefly struggle. A breeze, hot and heavy as a tired dog's breath, coated the web and fly with dust. I shaded my eyes and squinted down the road. Empty. As usual. It was almost two years since I'd seen anything but Jud's truck on Peachtree.

Like last month, and the month before that, and the third day of every month since I'd been out here alone, I squashed the fear that maybe this time he wouldn't come. But he always did come, rolling up in the cloud of dust he'd collected on the twenty-mile drive from Atlanta.

I turned my attention back to the fly. It kept right on struggling. I wondered how it felt, fighting something that didn't resist but just drained the life from it. It would take a long time to die. Like humankind.

The fly had stopped fighting by the time I heard Jud's truck. I didn't get up and brush myself off, he'd be few minutes yet; sound travels a long way when there's nothing filling the air but bird song.

He had someone with him. I sighed. Usually, Jud would give me a ride back down to the apartment. Looked like I'd have to walk this time: the truck was only a two-seater. It pulled up and Jud and another man, about twenty-eight I'd guess, maybe a couple of years younger than me, swung open their doors.

"How are you, Molly?" He climbed down, economical as always with his movements.

"Same as usual, Jud. Glad to see you." I nodded at the supplies and the huge gasoline drums in the back of the truck. "A day later and the generator would've been sucking air."

He grinned. "You're welcome." His partner walked around the front of the truck. Jud gestured. "This is Henry." Henry nodded. Like Jud, like me, he wore shorts, sneakers, and tee-shirt.

Jud didn't say why Henry was along for the ride, but I could guess: a relapse could hit anybody, anytime, leave you too exhausted even to keep the gas pedal down. I hoped Henry was just Jud's insurance and not another piece in the chess game he and I played from time to time.

"Step up if you want a ride," Jud said.

I looked questioningly at Henry.

"I can climb up into the back," he said. I watched him haul himself over the tailgate and hunker down by a case of tuna. Showing off. He'd pay for the exertion later. I shrugged, his problem, and climbed up into the hot vinyl seat.

Jud handled the truck gently, turning into the apartment complex as carefully as though five hundred people still lived here. The engine noise startled the nuthatches nesting in the postal center into a flurry of feathers; they perched on the roof and watched us pull up ten yards in, at what had been the clubhouse. I remember when the brass Westwater Terraces sign had been shined up every week: only three years ago. Six months after I'd first moved in people had begun to slow down and die off, and the management had added a few things, like the ramps and generator, to try and keep those who were left. It felt like a lifetime ago. I was the only one still here.

"Tiger lilies are looking good," Jud said. They were, straggling big and busy and orange all around the club-house; a feast for birds and bees.

The gasoline drums were lashed down, to stop them moving around the flatbed during the drive to Duluth. Henry untied the first and trundled it forward until it rested by the tailgate.

Inside the clubhouse the dark was hot and moist; a roach whirred when I uncoiled the hose. Back out in the sun I blew through it to clear any other insects, and spat into the dust. I put one end in the first drum.

I always hated the first suck but this time I was lucky and avoided a mouthful of gas. We didn't speak while the drums drained. It was an unseasonable May: over ninety degrees and humid as hell. Just standing was tiring.

"I don't mind walking the rest," I said to Henry.

"No need." He pulled himself back up into the flat-bed. More slowly this time. I didn't bother wasting my energy telling him not to use up his trying to impress a woman who was not in the least bit interested.

Jud started up the truck then let it coast the twenty yards down the slope to the apartment building I was using. When he cut the engine, we just sat there, listening to it tick, unwilling to step down and start the hauling around of cases that would leave us aching and tired for a week. Jud and I had worked out a routine long ago: I would go and get the trolley; he would unbolt the tailgate and slide out the ramp; he'd lift cases onto the trolley; I'd trundle them into the apartment. About halfway through we'd stop for iced tea, then swap chores and finish up.

This time, when I went to get the trolley, it was Henry who rattled the bolts on the tailgate and manhandled the ramp down from the flatbed in a squeal of metal. I did my third of the lifting and carrying, but it felt all wrong.

When we were done, and the cans of tuna and tomato and cat food, the sacks of flour and beans, the packets and cases and bottles and tins were all heaped in the middle of the living room floor and we'd bolted the tailgate back up, I invited them both into the cool apartment for iced tea. We sat. Henry wiped his face with a bandanna and sipped.

"That's good on a dusty throat, Ms. O'Connell."

"Molly."

He nodded acknowledgement. I felt Jud watching, and waited for the inevitable. "Nice place you have here, Molly. Jud tells me you've stayed here on your own for almost three years." It was closer to two since Helen died, but I let that pass. "You ever had any accidents?"

"One or two, nothing I couldn't handle."

"Bet they gave you a scare. Imagine if you broke your leg or somesuch: no phone, nobody for twenty miles around to help. A person could die out here." His tanned face looked earnest, concerned, and his eyes were very blue. I looked at Jud, who shrugged: he hadn't put him up to this.

"I'm safe enough," I said to Henry.

He caught my tone and didn't say anything more right away. He looked around again, searching for a neutral subject, nodded at the computer. "You use that a lot?"

"Yes."

Jud decided to take pity on him. "Molly's writing a book. About how all this happened, and what we know about the disease so far."

"Syndrome," I corrected.

Jud's mouth crooked in a half smile. "See how knowledgeable she is?" He drained his glass, hauled himself off the couch, and refilled it in the kitchen. Henry and I did not speak until he got back to the couch.

In the past, Jud had tried everything: teasing me about being a misanthrope; trying to make me feel guilty about how the city had to waste valuable resources sending me supplies every month; raging at my selfishness. This time he just tilted his head to one side and looked sad.

"We need you, Molly."

I said nothing. We'd been through this before: he thought I might be able to find a way to cure the syndrome; I told him I hadn't much chance of succeeding where a decade of intense research had failed. I didn't blame him for trying—I was probably one of the last immunologists alive—it's just that I didn't think I could do anything to help: I and the world's best had already beaten our heads bloody against that particular brick wall and gotten nowhere. I'd done everything I could, and I'd had a very good reason to try achieve the impossible.

I had tried everything I knew, followed every avenue of enquiry, run down every lead. Working with support and good health, with international cooperation and resources, I got nowhere: my promising leads led to nothing, my time ran out, and Helen died. What did they think I could achieve now, on my own?

They'd told me, once, that they would take me into Atlanta forcibly. I said: fine, do that, see how far it gets you. Coercion might make me go through the motions, but that's all. Good research demands commitment. Stalemate. But the way they saw it, I was their only hope, and maybe I would change my mind.

"Why do you stay?" Henry said into the silence.

I shrugged. "I like it here."

"No," Jud said slowly, "you stay because you still like to pretend that the rest of the world is getting on fine, that if you don't see that Atlanta is a ghost town you won't have to believe it, believe any of this is real."

"Maybe you're right," I said lightly, "but I'm still not leaving."

I stood, and went to rinse my glass. If the people of Atlanta wanted to bring me food and precious gasoline in an attempt to keep me alive until I changed my mind, I wasn't going to feel guilty. I wasn't going to change my mind either. Humanity might be dying, but I saw no reason why we should struggle, just for the sake of struggling, when it would do no good. I am not a cranefly.

·⟡·

I woke up briefly in the middle of the night to the soft sound of rain and the eerie chorus of bullfrogs. Even after two years I still slept curled up on one side of the bed; I still woke expecting to see her silhouette.

My arms and hips ached. I ran a hot bath and soaked for a while, until I got too hot, then went back to bed where I lay on my back and did chi kung breathing. It helped. The song of bullfrogs steadied into a ratchety rhythm. I slept.

·⟡·

When I woke the sky was still red in the east. The bedroom window no longer opened so I padded stiffly through to the living room and slid open the door onto the deck. The air was cool enough for spring. I leaned on my elbows and looked out across the creek; the blind-eyed buildings on the other side of the gully were hidden by white swamp oaks that stretched their narrow trunks up into a sky the same powder blue as a bluebird's wing. To the right, sun gleamed on the lake. Birds sang, too many to identify. A cardinal flashed through the trees.

My world. I didn't want anything else. Jud was partially right: why should I want to live in Atlanta among people as sick as myself, listen to them groan when they woke up in the morning with stiff knees and stomach cramps, watch them walk slowly, like geriatrics, when I had all this? The birds weren't sick; the trees did not droop; every spring there were thousands of tadpoles in the pond. And none of them depended on me, none of them looked at me with hope in their eyes. Here, I was just me, just Molly, part of a world that offered no pain, no impossible challenge.

I went inside, but left the door open to the air and bird song. I moved jerkily, because my hips still hurt, and because I was angry with all those like Jud who wanted to fight and fight to their last breath. Humankind was dying. It didn't take a rocket scientist to figure that out: if women had so little strength that they died not long after childbirth, then the population would inevitably dwindle. Only five or six generations before humanity reached vanishing point.

I wanted to enjoy what I could of it; I wanted to write this book so that those who were born, if they survived the guilt of their mother's death, would at least understand their doom. We might not understand the passing of the dinosaurs, but we should understand our own.

After breakfast I put on some Bach harpsichord music and sat down at the keyboard. I pulled up Chapter Three, full of grim statistics, and looked it over. Not today. I exited, called up Chapter One: How It All Began. I wrote about Helen.

We'd been living here at Westwater Terraces for two months. I remember the brutal heat of the August move. We swore that next time we had to carry desks and packing cases, we'd make sure it was in March, or October. Helen loved it here. I'd get home from the lab after a twenty-minute drive, and she'd bring me iced tea and tell me all about how the fish in the lake—she called it the pond, too small for a lake, she said—were growing, or about the turtle she saw on her lunchtime walk and the way a squirrel had filled its mouth with nuts, and she'd ease away all the heat and snarl of a hard day's work and the Mad Max commute. The pond was her inspiration—all those wonderful studies of light and shadow that hang on people's walls—her comfort when a show went badly or a gallery refused to exhibit. I rarely bothered to walk by the pond myself, content to see it through her eyes.

Then she won the competition, and we flew to Bali—for the green and the sealight, she said—on the proceeds. I was grateful for those precious weeks we had in Bali.

When we got home, she was tired. The tiredness got worse. Then she began to hurt, her arms, her knees, her elbows. We assumed it was some kind of flu, and I pampered her for a while. But instead of getting better, she got worse: headaches, nausea, rashes on her face and arms. Moving too fast made her lower body go numb. When I realized she hadn't been around the pond for nine days, I knew she was very sick.

We went to the doctor who had diagnosed my gastroenteritis the year before She suggested Helen had Chronic Fatigue Syndrome. We did some reading. The diagnosis was a blow, and a relief. The Syndrome had many names—Myalgic Encephalomyelitis, Chronic Fatigue Syndrome, Chronic Epstein-Barr, Post Viral Fatigue Syndrome, Chronic Immune Dysfunction, Yuppie Flu—but no clear pattern, no cure. Doctors scratched their heads over it, but then said not to worry: it was self-limiting, and there had been no known deaths.

We saw four different doctors, who prescribed everything from amino-acid supplements to antibiotics to breathing and meditation. The uncertain leading the ignorant. Most agreed that she would be well again, somehow, in two or three years.

There were weeks when Helen could not get out of bed, or even feed herself. Then there were weeks when we argued, taking turns to alternately complain that she did too much, or not enough. In one three-month period, we did not make love once. Then Helen found out about a support group, and for a while we felt positive, on top of things.

Then people with CFS began to die.

No one knew why. They just got worse over a period of weeks until they were too weak to breathe. Then others became infected with a variation of the syndrome: the course of the disease was identical, but the process accelerated. Death usually occurred a month or so after the first symptom.

Helen died here, the day the Canada geese came. She was lying on the couch, one hand in mine, the other curled loosely around Jessica, who was purring by her hip. It was Jessica who heard the geese first. She stopped purring and lifted her head, ears pricked. Then I heard them too, honking to each other like they owned the world. They arrowed past, necks straining, wings going like the north wind, and white cheeks orangy yellow in the evening sun. Helen tried to sit up to look.

They circled the lake a couple of times before skimming in to land. Their wake was still slapping up against the bridge posts when Helen died. I sat there a long time, holding her hand, glad that she'd heard the geese.

They woke me at dawn the next day, honking and crying to each other through the trees on their way to wherever. I lay and listened to the silence they left behind, realized it would always be silent now: I would never hear Helen breathe beside me again. Jessica mewed and jumped up onto the bed; I stroked her, grateful for her mindless warmth and affection.

I came home tired from the funeral, with that bone-deep weariness that only comes from grief. Or so I thought. It took me almost a week to realize I was sick too.

The disease spread. No one knew the vector, because still no one was sure what the agent was: viral, bacterial, environmental, genetic? The spread was slow. There was plenty of time for planning by local and national bodies. It was around this time that we got the generator at the complex: the management were still thinking in terms of weathering the crisis, persuading occupants that it was safe for them to stay, that even if the city power failed, and the water systems, they'd be fine here.

There's something about the human race: as it slowly died, those that were left became more needy of each other. It seemed that we all became a little kinder, too. Everyone pulled inward, to the big cities where there was food, and power, and sewage systems. I stayed where I was. I figured I'd die soon, anyway, and I had this irrational urge to get to know the pond.

So I stayed, but I didn't die. And gradually it became clear that not everyone did. The latest count indicated that almost five percent of the world's population has survived. The deaths have been slow and inevitable enough that those of us who are still here have been able to train ourselves to do whatever it takes to stay alive. It wasn't so hard to keep things going: when the population is so small, it's surprising how many occupations become redundant. Insurance clerks now work in the power stations; company executives check sewage lines; police officers drive threshing machines. No one works more than four hours a day; we don't have the strength. None of us shows any signs of recovering. None but the most foolish still believe we will.

<hr />

Westwater Terraces is built around a small lake and creek. Behind the water, to the west, are deciduous woods; other trees in the complex are a mix of conifers and hardwoods: white pine and oak, birch and yellow poplar. The apartment buildings are connected by gravel paths; three white-painted bridges span a rivulet, the creek, and the western end of the lake.

I stood on the bridge over the rivulet, the one Helen and I had always called the Billy Goats' Gruff bridge, and called for Jessica. Weeds and sycamore saplings pushed through the gravel path to my left; a dead oak straddled the path further up. Strong sun made the cat food in the dish by my feet smell unpleasantly.

The paint on the bridge was peeling. While I waited, I picked at it and wondered idly why paint always weathered in a pattern resembling a cross-section of epithelial cells, and why the wood always turned silvery gray.

Today I missed Jessica fiercely, missed the warmth of her on my lap and her fur tickling my nose when I tried to read. I hadn't seen her for over a week; sometimes the cat food I put out was eaten, sometimes it wasn't. A warbler landed on the bridge and cocked its head, close enough for me to see the gleam of its bright eye and the fine wrinkles on the joints of its feet.

I waited longer than usual, but she didn't come. I scrunched over the gravel feeling annoyed with myself for needing to hold another warm living creature.

Late morning was edging towards noon and the sun was hot on my shoulders. I was thirsty, too, but didn't want to go back to the beige walls of my apartment just yet.

The lake used to have three fountains. One still works, which I regard as a minor miracle. A breeze pulled cool, moist air off the surface of the water and through my hair. A frog plopped out of sight, warned of my approach by the vibration of my footsteps. The ripple of its passing disturbed the duckweed and the water lilies. They were open to the light: white, pink, yellow. A bee hummed over the rich yellow anthers and I wondered if any ever got trapped when the lilies closed in the afternoon.

The bridge spanning the thinner, western end of the lake was roofed, a kind of watery gazebo reigned over by spiders. I crossed carefully, watchful of their webs. Helen used to call it running the gauntlet; some of the webs stretched five feet in diameter, and very few were empty.

For me, the bridge was a divide between two worlds. The lake lay on the left, the east, a wide open expanse reflecting the blue sky, rippling with fountain water, surrounded by white pine and yellow iris. The right, the western end, was the pond: green and secret, shrouded by frog-bit and lily pads. Stickleback and carp hung in the shadow of cattails and reeds, finning cool water over their scales.

There are almost a dozen ducks here, mallards mostly. And their ducklings. Careful of webs, I leaned on the rail to watch. The one with the right wing sticking up at a painful angle was paddling slowly toward a weeping willow on the left bank. Two of her three ducklings hurried after her. I wondered where the other one was.

It was getting too hot to be out.

Walking around the other side of the lake to get back to the roadway was hard work. The ground sloped steeply and the heat was getting fierce. Storms brought heavy rains in the summer and they were gradually washing away the dirt path, making it unsafe in places. The lake was twenty-five, maybe thirty, feet below me now and to my left, partially screened by the trees and undergrowth on the sloping bank. I heard a peeping noise from the water, just behind a clump of arrowhead. Maybe it was the missing duckling. I stepped near to the edge to get a closer look.

I felt the bucket-size clump of dirt give and slide from under my left foot, but my leg muscles, already tired from the heat and the climb, couldn't adapt to the sudden shift. My body weight dropped to one side with nothing to hold it but bone and ligament. I felt the ligament tear and pop and bones grind together. Then I fell, rolling and sliding down the slope, pain like a hot rock in my stomach.

I crashed into the knobbed bark of an oak; it took the skin off my back and shoulder. I saw the mossy rock clearly just before I hit it.

I woke to heat thick enough to stand on. My mouth was very dry and my cheek hurt. My face was pressed against a tree root. I blinked and tried to sit up. The world swooped sickeningly. This time my face fell on grass. It felt better at first, not so hard.

I was hurt. Concussion at least. Something crawled down my cheek and into my ear. It took me a moment to realize it was a tear; it felt like someone else was crying, not me. I closed my eyes and began my testing with the left leg, moving it just an inch or so. More tears squeezed out from under my eyelids: the ankle and knee felt like they were being cut into with a rusty ripsaw. I moved my right leg. That was fine. My left arm seemed all in one piece, but moving the right hurt my ribs. I remembered hitting the tree. Probably just bruising.

I opened my eyes. The tree root my face had been resting on belonged to a smooth-barked birch. If I was sitting up I might be able to think.

I pulled my right leg under me and pulled myself forward with my left elbow. My moan startled a lizard sunning itself behind a leafy clump of purple loosestrife; its belly flashed blue as it skittered through the undergrowth and disappeared into a rotting tree stump. Sweat wormed over my scraped ribs, stinging. I dragged myself forward again.

I had to lift my head, bring my right elbow down to hip level and twist to roll over onto my back. The pain and the dizziness pulled thick, stringy nausea up over my skin. I thought I was going to pass out. After a moment, I sat up, shuffled back a couple of feet, and leaned against the tree.

The sun shone almost directly into my eyes. The floating sunlotus were open now, damselflies flashing metallic blues and greens against the rich yellow cups: must be about three o'clock in the afternoon. The air was still and quiet; the frogs silent, and the birds sleepy. Fountain water pattered and splashed. I was very thirsty, and the air felt too hot and big in my lungs.

The slope stretched more than twenty feet upward to the path. I could do it if I moved in a zig-zag and used every tree for support, and if I started soon: I was dehydrated and every moment I spent out in the sun made it worse. The water was about ten feet away, downslope, almost hidden by the tangle of ivy, undergrowth and dead wood.

I edged myself around the bole of the birch and shuffled backwards. The next closest tree was a white pine, about five feet away to the right. I had to stop four times before I got to within touching distance of the pine. I rested against its trunk, panting. The bark was rough and smelled of sun-warmed resin.

It was taking too long: at this rate, the sun would have leached away all my strength before I got even halfway up the slope. I had to risk moving faster. That meant standing up.

I wrapped my arms around the trunk and got myself onto my right knee. The soil was cool and damp on my bare skin. I hauled myself up. The ridged trunk glided in and out of focus.

The next tree was close, only two feet directly up-slope. Trying not to think how easy this would be if both legs worked, I took a deep breath and hopped.

The world came crashing down around my head.

I opened my eyes. The pool was slicked with sunset, hot and dark and mysterious. Whirligigs and waterboatmen dimpled the surface. My hand hung in the water. I pulled my face forward a few inches and lapped. Some went up my nose and dribbled down my chin, but enough went into my mouth to swallow a couple of times.

I drank again. It tasted odd, thin and green, but I could feel the good it was doing me. My cheeks felt hot and tight: sunburn. I dipped one side of my face in the water, then the other, then rested my forehead on my arm. Cicadas filled the evening with their chitinous song.

It looked like I'd been out four hours or more. No point beating myself over the head with my stupidity. The best thing I could do for myself right now was rest, wait for the coolth of night, rehydrate. Then think.

Swallows dipped and skimmed over the center of the lake, drinking in flight, snipping up unwary insects with wing-flicking grace. A cotton mouse nosed her way out from under a pile of leaves and scampered from the shelter of a log to a tree root. She sat up and gnawed on a seed.

I tried not to think about the green peppers ripening on the slope behind my apartment, of the fish in the freezer and fruit in the refrigerator.

About two feet away, a big spider sat on a lily pad, perfectly still but for one of its back legs that hung in the water, twitching. I thought maybe the leg was trapped by something, some hidden weed, but the rhythm was too deliberate; the spider was using the surface of the water as a drum. A mosquito fish came to investigate. It was tiny, no longer than a fingernail. The spider shot out its front legs and hauled the fish onto the lily pad, into its mouth.

The sunset had turned to purple and I could see stars. Tonight I couldn't recognize any of them; they looked cold and alien. It was cooling rapidly now, but I made no attempt to sit up.

My concussion and exhaustion had prompted a poor decision earlier: heading upslope was not the only way. If I could see a route along the lake shore that was relatively clear of undergrowth, I could walk or crawl around it until I reached the eastern end where the bank was only four or five feet high. That route would also bring me closer to the roadway that led to the apartment.

I blinked. I'd been asleep: the moon was up. This time, I could dip my hand into the water and bring it to my mouth to drink. I felt less like a wounded animal, more like a thinking, reasoning human being.

47

All around the pond, bullfrogs were singing. The moon was bright enough to reflect the flutter of trapped wings four feet from where I lay: perfectly still, a frog sat half hidden by cattails, a caddisfly in its mouth. The fly stopped struggling; they only lived a few hours anyway. Born without mouths, they reproduced then died. The frog's eyes glittered cold in the moonlight, watching me. Bullfrogs lived fifteen years.

They sang louder, following each other's lead, altering duration, pitch, and rhythm until the water boomed and echoed with their song. Tree frogs buzzed in the higher registers. I felt surrounded and menaced by sound.

Leaves rustled; a shadow eased through the undergrowth behind me. I turned my head slowly, faced two green eyes like headlights. Jessica. A friendly face.

"Jess. Here baby." She sniffed at my hip. I patted my chest, an invitation for her to snuggle. She froze. "Come on Jess. Come here baby." She sniffed my hand, and purred. I laughed. "Yes, you wild thing. It's me." Your friend.

She licked my hand. I lifted it to stroke her. She hissed. "It's me, Jess. Me." She regarded me with cold emerald eyes; in the moonlight, her teeth looked like old ivory.

A small creature, maybe the cotton mouse, scuttled somewhere close to the water. Jessica crouched, bellied forward.

I remembered how she had looked as a seven-week old kitten, the way she had comforted me when Helen died.

Now I saw her as she had always been: a hunter, a wildcat who only licked my hand for the salt. I was not part of her world. I was not any part of anything's world. What I saw when I looked into the eyes of a frog or a mouse was nothing: not fear, not affection, not even contempt.

But I stayed. For Helen. To be part of the world Helen had loved. But staying here did not make me part of Helen's world: Helen was dead. Gone. She'd gone and left

48

me with nothing. No one. It wasn't fair. I didn't want to be alone.

I beat on the dirt with my fist. Why had she died and left me alone? Why? Why, Helen?

"Tell me why!"

My scream was raw, too hot, too human for this place. Tears rolled down my cheeks, big tears, big enough to reflect the world a new way. Helen was gone, and the geese were gone; I could stay here forever and she would never come back. I shouldn't be here.

The realization made me feel remote, very calm.

I sat up, ignoring the pain. Getting my tee-shirt off was difficult; stretching for the branch two feet away, even worse. The tee-shirt was already ripped; it made it easier for me to tear it into strips. I had to try several times before I could tie secure knots around the makeshift splint. Whenever the pain got too much, I rested.

An owl hooted, hunting.

I levered myself up onto knee and elbows, left leg stuck out behind me, stiff in its splint. Pain was just pain.

I dragged myself forward through a monochrome world: water sleek and black; trumpet honeysuckle leached lithium gray; moonlight lying like pools of mercury on leaves the color of graphite. Nature, thinking there was no one there to observe, let slide the greens and purples, the honey yellows, and showed her other face: flat, indifferent, anonymous.

I imagined making my pain as impersonal as nature's night face, putting it in a pouch at the small of my back, zipping the pouch shut. Out of sight, out of mind. Somewhere, I knew, there was a place where all the colors and scents of the day waited for morning, and then I would smell iris and pine resin, rich red dirt and green pond scum. And feel the hot orange jags of pain. In the morning.

Right elbow, right knee, left elbow, drag. I focused on the tree forty yards away on the eastern bank, the tree I would use to haul myself upright and up onto the road. Right elbow, right knee, left elbow, drag.

Behind me, I heard the squeak of a small animal. The cotton mouse. Right elbow, right knee, left elbow, drag. The night stretched on.

The tree bark was rough on hands and arms already red raw. No pain until morning. I pulled myself up the incline. The road felt marvelously smooth. I lay my cheek on the asphalt and breathed in the smell of dust and artificial things. Below, the pond glimmered, obsidian. The bullfrogs sang.

My ankle was not broken. I suspected that several ligaments were torn, in my ankle and knee, but distalgesics and support bandages kept me able to manage until, eight days later, I could get around using a heavy branch as a cane. It was hard to hold the cane: the bandages wrapped around my hands and forearms were thick and clumsy.

I limped out to the deck and lowered myself into the hammock: the sky was thick with churning clouds. Usually, I loved watching the sheer power of a storm, the way it could boom and slash and drive over a hot and parched world, cooling and soaking. This time it was different. This time, when the wind tore through the stand of swamp white oak, it seemed to me that it was killing things, flattening them, exposing them: turning the oak leaves silvery side up, ripping off branches, bending the trees almost to breaking point, pressing the grasses flat to the earth and snapping the heads off the marsh marigold. It was brutal.

I swung myself off the hammock. The show could go on without me. Inside, I made myself hot tea, put on Vivaldi—human music to drown the sound of the storm— and retired to the couch with a book, facing away from the glass doors. Let it do what it wanted. I refused to watch the rain swell the creek until it rose high enough to fill the burrows of voles and mice and drown their young.

My ankle and knee improved and I could walk slowly without the cane. I took the bandages off my arms. I did not go near the pond, and walked only on the black artificial surfaces of the road.

Tonight was soft and warm, there was a quarter moon. I walked over the Billy Goats' Gruff bridge and listened to the frogs singing around the pond. I turned and walked up to the clubhouse. It took me a while to find the red switch handle. I threw it; the floodlight still worked.

I stood on the road overlooking the pond. Sodium light heaved greasily on the water next to the silver ripple of the moon. The water looked mysterious, unknowable, like an ancient harbour lit by naphtha flaming in a great bronze bowl.

I looked at it a long time. Helen was not here, she was in my heart. The pond belonged to the past.

I waited by the side of the road for Jud. There were more flowers, and it was just as hot and dusty, but this time there was no spider web, no cranefly. Just the birds singing, and me sitting on my suitcase. Three of Helen's paintings, wrapped in our sheets, leaned against the gate.

Jud was on his own. He coasted the truck to a stop and climbed down. I stood. He saw the suitcase.

"This mean what I think it means?"

"Yes."

And that's all we said. He always did know when to speak and when to keep quiet. He helped me push the case and the paintings up into the back, in among all the cans and bottles and sacks I wouldn't be needing.

"You want to drive?" he asked. I shook my head. We climbed up. I put the seatbelt on; my life had suddenly become more precious. Jud noticed, but said nothing. He made a U-turn and we set off back along the road to Atlanta.

I leaned my head against the window and watched the dog violets nodding at the side of the road. I had nearly died out here, believing struggling was for fools and craneflies. Perhaps those who struggled were fools, but they were fools with hope. They were human. Helen was dead. I was not. I was sick, yes, but I still had intelligence, direction, purpose. And time. Something craneflies did not have. If I personally could not finish the research I intended, then those who came after me would. I could teach them what I learned; they would build on it. If I struggled and failed, that was not the end. I am not a cranefly.

▓ *Yaguara*

Jane Holford valued her privacy. That is why she became a photographer: people would look at her pictures and not at her. As an adolescent she had watched a film critic on television. *The gaze of the camera is not like grammar*, he had said. *After a while there is no difference between subject and object.* He pointed at a still of Marilyn Monroe, dead for years. *We ate her alive.* Jane had decided then and there that she would be neither subject nor object but invulnerable *observer*. She would keep herself armored, inviolate, safe.

And so Jane did not travel directly from England to Belize. She packed her cameras and flew to the Yucatan, and from there took a boat to Ambergris Cay. She would acclimatize to the heat slowly, and in private.

On Ambergris, Katherine—the ex-governor's niece for whom Jane had once done the favor of losing a roll of incriminating film—was drunk by ten o'clock in the morning and forgot, most of the time, that she had a guest, and the house servants probably could not have cared less. But Jane still maintained a perfect control. Even when the sun was licking at her shoulders and the Caribbean wove about her its scents of wide-open space and hot driftwood, she did not throw back her head and laugh; she did not take off her sandals and squeeze the seaweed between her toes. When a beautiful woman in the market smiled at her, she did not smile back, did not allow herself to blush, to feel the heat building in her belly.

Alone in her room, it was another matter.

After three weeks she no longer felt vulnerable: she could walk outside in the sun without fainting; she knew how much water she needed to drink every day to remain hydrated; and her skin was dark enough to protect her from sunburn. Armor in place, she left for the Maya Mountains in the far south and west of Belize. Dr. Cleis Fernandez and the ruins of Kuchil Balum were waiting.

"Why do you want to take pictures of me?" the epigrapher had asked when Jane had phoned the University of New Mexico a month earlier, at the beginning of March.

"Because I'm putting together a book on women at the top of their professions." *Because you made it, against the odds. Because you haven't let them consume you, yet.* "You're—"

"Get someone else." And the phone had gone dead in Jane's hand.

Jane re-dialed. "Dr. Fernandez, it's Jane Holford again—"

"Wait a minute. Holford? Holford who did that series last year on the Lascaux paintings? The ones in *Life*?"

"Yes." At last. "And I might excerpt a similar photo-essay from the book in one of the glossies—"

"I'm not interested in that." Her voice was hot and rough, like black glass. "But I do have one condition."

"Go on."

"I want you to photograph the glyphs at Kuchil Balum."

"Tell me about them."

"It's classified as a minor ceremonial site in Belize but it's anything but minor. As for the rest . . . well, you'll come or you won't."

"I'll call you back."

She had checked. Kuchil Balum was in the Maya Mountains, first excavated two years before. Nothing there that could not be found in dozens of other, more accessible ruins in Belize or Guatemala. And yet… Apparently Fernandez had been applying for grants all over the place, for money and time to go study these ruins and their glyphs. She had been turned down. Jane read and re-read Fernandez's articles in the journals, and *The Long Count*, her single book. The passion and dedication, the need to know, came across loud and clear. Why was Kuchil Balum so important?

She called back four days after their original conversation. "I'll do it."

"You will?" Fernandez sounded challenging. "The jungle isn't a good place just before the rainy season."

"I understand that. Now, my schedule—"

"I'm going there next week and won't be coming out again until the rainy season, May or June. Take it or leave it."

The road was a track torn through the tropical forest by logging skidders, deteriorating to dust and potholes and broken bridges. Leaves brushed the jeep on both sides and smeared the dusty paintwork with sap, leaving Jane with the feeling that the greenery was closing in behind her and she would be encysted in the forest forever.

Not long after noon, she stopped to drink water from her canteen and eat a banana. It was hot; mosquitoes and bottlas flies whined about her head. Wind, sly as a great cat's breath, stole from banak to ironwood to Santa Maria pine, stirring hot perfumes and the iridescent wings of a blue morpho butterfly. When she turned the key in the ignition, the jeep's engine roared too loudly, and it seemed to Jane that when she moved, the breath of the forest followed.

Over an hour later, the jungle ahead of her thinned abruptly, melting from dense emerald to sunlit mint. The breeze stiffened and expelled her into a green-sided bowl floored with dirt-brown: a clearing. Adobe huts roofed with thatch stood in an irregular west-east line; a macaw hung in a cage outside the nearest. Chickens scratched in the dirt, and a pig rooted in the undergrowth at the edge of the clearing. She turned off the engine and found herself staring into the solemn eyes of a group of thin-armed children.

Stranger, those unblinking camera eyes said, *you cannot hide.*

One child wiped his nose with the back of his hand, another tilted her head at Jane like a bird. Then at some unseen signal they ran like a pack of startled deer back towards the forest and melted into the trees.

Jane climbed down from the jeep and began to lift an aluminum case from the back.

"Don't do that."

She whirled, found herself facing a lean woman wearing shorts and boots and vest; muscles showing long and tight over knobby bones; neck tendons flat and hard; face planed by heat and hard work; hair in rough curls as black as volcanic rock.

"I'm Cleis Fernandez." When they shook hands, Cleis's long fingers reached past Jane's wrist. "It would be best to leave your things in the jeep. It's another half mile or so to our shack. We can drive if we go very, very slowly."

Our shack. She had prepared for everything but sharing a room. Jane climbed numbly back into the jeep.

Jane knew she drove well: poised, unhurried, competent. She glanced in the side mirror, caught the flash of brown eyes studying her in turn, and deliberately looked away. She was the observer, not the observed.

"This is it." It was a square building of breeze block and corrugated aluminum. They climbed down. "It was built by the logging company. Never got used—they went bust. It's more comfortable inside than it looks."

A wooden step led into a single room, low and dark, about eighteen feet square, with plasterboard walls and a dirt floor. There were wooden-framed bunks, each with a blue blanket.

Two bunks. No room into which she could retreat and close the door.

"There's a toilet over here," Cleis pointed, "though I, we, have to fill the cistern from a bucket. The well's in the village; Ixbalum lets me, us, use that at least. The stove uses propane." She lit a match, turned a knob, demonstrated. "I cleared some of the shelf space for your things."

Jane looked at the clothes already on the shelf. They looked new. Aggressively good quality. She had seen clothes like that before, when she had shared a room at Cambridge with a scholarship girl.

The windows were holes cut in the wall and screened, the door a flimsy affair. Jane looked for a lock.

"No one will steal anything. Ixbalum won't even let anyone near this place." Jane nodded, wondering who Ixbalum was. "We've got three Coleman lamps...."

Jane closed her eyes. Sharing. The hut smelled of heat and mildew and sweat, and faintly of gas and matches, but behind that lay the must of forest animals and the heavy green scent of ceaseless growth. She felt trapped.

"...last as long as possible, because I hate the drive to Benque Viejo for more supplies, though if you're willing, we can take turns on that chore. Jane?"

She opened her eyes, smiled her warm, practiced smile. "Thank you for going to so much trouble." *How am I going to survive this?*

The well was at the western edge of the village. Jane wound up the bucket. "Where is everyone?"

"Tending their milpas. Or hunting. Some are hiding in their houses. The children are running wild, or maybe watching us right now."

Jane could see only trees and the inevitable chickens.

The bucket creaked to the lip of the well. Jane concentrated on pouring from the wooden bucket into the galvanized steel pail. She was fascinated by the cool clear flow, the fact that water could stay cold in one hundred-degree heat. She dipped her hand in it.

Someone behind her spoke in a throaty Mayan dialect. Jane turned, saw a short, muscular woman with squat powerful limbs and a large jaw.

"Jane, this is Ixbalum."

"What did she say?"

"That rivers are for playing with, well water for drinking."

Ixbalum lifted Jane's left arm, laid it next to her own, pointed to the mahogany brown then the honey, dropped the arm, lifted Cleis's arm, compared the mahogany to teak, spoke for a while, then padded away into the trees.

Jane realized she was wiping her hands on her shorts, stopped. "What did she say?"

"She said you're not made for the mountains."

It was just over a mile from the village to the ruins. The trail was a twisty tunnel through the green. Sweat ran down the underside of Jane's arm, and she felt as though she were breathing sap. Ahead of her, Cleis's shorts whif-whiffed as she walked. Their boots were silent on the thick leaf mold. Insects hummed and whined. Jane slapped at something that landed on her neck.

"Got to be careful of the insects," Cleis said over her shoulder without slowing down. "Especially mosquitoes. They carry botfly eggs and things out of your worst nightmares." Cleis had no idea about her nightmares, Jane thought.

They walked on in silence. The heat pushed its strong fingers under Jane's skin, slicked muscle and bone until she felt slippery inside, like a well-oiled machine. The jungle eased down her throat, sighed in her ears, whispered *You could let go here, and no one would know.*

Jane realized she was stroking her belly, walking with a loose, open-hip sway. *Armored, inviolate, safe . . .* She jerked her hand away from her stomach and laid it on the hard black case hanging down by her hip. She was the only one with a camera here. She was in control.

Cleis stopped abruptly, turned. "We're almost there. You have to remember that this is classified as a minor site, not to be confused with the great centers like Tikal." Cleis's hands moved as she talked, emphasizing phrases with precise gestures like movements distilled from tai chi or wing chun. "There's only one pyramid, and that hasn't been fully excavated. Nothing has. It may not look like much but Kuchil Balum is more important than anyone knows." Her hands stopped, fell back to her sides. "I just wanted you to know that."

They climbed the last few yards up a steep rise and looked down at Kuchil Balum.

Grassy hummocks and walls choked with vines lay scattered around an area the size of a small urban park, perhaps two acres, level, but slightly sunken. It reminded Jane of the huge ruined amphitheaters of Greece, only here it was wood, not stone, that formed the sides of the bowl; great vertigo-producing trunks that spun themselves up and up to bridge earth and heaven.

Over the faint susurrus of leaves a hundred feet from the ground, Jane thought she heard something else, something that she felt as a faint vibration under her feet. "What's that noise?"

Cleis smiled. "We'll save that for last."

Jane clambered over a pile of tumbled stone and to the top of a small mound. It was not hard to envisage this place as it had once been: people coming and going, sun flashing on jade and gold; children playing with a ball. Why had they left?

The northwestern corner of the site was hemmed in by gray rock. In front of that lay a whole complex of ruins. Something just inside the trees caught her attention, something golden that slunk from light to shadow, lifting heavy paws, turning its massive head from side to side. Slowly, heart hammering under her ribs, Jane lifted her camera.

"What is it?"

The golden animal was gone. Perhaps she had imagined it. Jane lowered her camera. "Nothing."

"Over here is the mat house." They walked back down the slope to a small green mound with one side exposed: a few gray stones, beautifully fitted, a doorway and lintel. "I'm particularly interested in the glyphs on the western wall." They squeezed through. Inside it was dim and smelled of animal fur and musk, like a woman's hair after the rain. Cleis ran her hand along the wall. "This section here is vital." She tapped a relief carving, a seated jaguar-headed figure. "The throne indicates temporal power, but other indicators point to the human figure being female. That's very unusual." She looked at Jane. "About as usual as a Latina professor in your Anglo world."

Jane said nothing, refusing to be baited. Cleis smiled slightly, then continued. "Over here," she traced her way across the name glyphs and dates, "another jaguar-human, but this time not in the regalia of the royal house. See the scythe? A peasant. I've seen jaguars as thrones, jaguars as symbols of shamanic and from there royal power, but this is the first time I've seen jaguars as ordinary citizens, or vice versa. I don't know what it means." Frustration deepened the grooves on either side of her mouth for a moment, then she shook her head. "It's dark in here. I hope photographing them won't be a problem."

"No." Jane touched the glyphs lightly with her fingertips.

The strange, bulbous carvings were everywhere she and Cleis went. Cleis's hands were never still as she pointed out the date glyphs and name glyphs, explained the long count and the calendar round. She saved the northwest corner for last.

They climbed up the remains of four huge terraced steps and then through all that remained of what had once been a corridor. The vibration became a thrumming hiss. "See these hinges here? This corridor was once gated on both ends. Very unusual."

They stepped out into sunlight. Cold spray brushed Jane's cheek.

"A waterfall…" But Cleis did not give Jane long to admire the fall, or the pool bobbing with lilies. "This way." They went down steps cut into the stone, underground for five yards, then up again into what had once been a vast courtyard.

Cleis pointed to the wall that ran across the courtyard in six separate sections. It was covered in glyphs. "This is the heart of Kuchil Balum. This is why I'm here."

Jane posed Cleis at the well, at the ruins, outside the shack, trying to catch the intensity that seemed to burn at the woman's center. They stopped when the light faded.

At dusk the air tasted like hot metal. Jane sat on the step outside their shack and sipped at a battered tin cup: rum, lime juice and well water. Night light, Cleis called it. From inside, the galvanized pail clanked as the epigrapher flushed the toilet. Jane heard the laughter of children float up from the village.

"Not one child in that village has ever seen the inside of a school." Cleis filled her cup, sat next to Jane. "If only Ixbalum were willing to talk, the lack of education could be invaluable to me...."

Jane was glad to keep the conversation impersonal. "In what way?"

"Virtually all the schooling in Belize is done by missionaries: Catholics, Methodists, Seventh Day Adventists, the Assembly of God—you name it, they're here." She sipped meditatively. "There are probably three million people around today who still speak various Mayan tongues, but none of them can read these glyphs. The rituals that gave meaning to all these things were destroyed and discredited by the missionaries."

"But not here?"

"Not here. They probably still tell each other bedtime stories about Queen Jaguar Claw, and how she ruled over Mommy and Daddy's great-great-great to the nth-degree grandparents, and how she gave their children jade beads for...I don't know...maize productivity or something. But they won't talk to me. Ixbalum won't let them."

"I wonder what Ixbalum's afraid of."

Cleis was quiet for a long time. Plum-purple shadows gathered under her cheekbones and in the hollows of her neck. "That I'll make them famous."

Jane nodded slowly in the gathering dark. They had evaded notice for a long time. "How was Kuchil Balum discovered?"

"Three years ago a logger was tracking a jaguar. Came across some funny looking stones. He didn't think much of them at the time. Apparently he never did find the jaguar, but on the way back, he was bitten by a fer-de-lance. By the time his friends got him to the clinic at Benque

Viejo, he was bleeding from the eyes and babbling about a city of stone. He died a few hours later. But one of the nurses remembered what he'd said and told her friend. The friend knew someone who worked for the State Archaeology Department. They sent someone down, some idiot who took a cursory look, labelled it 'Minor Ceremonial Center,' and forgot about it. It was listed, of course, but these sites turn up all the time. Still, I was curious, I'm always curious, so when one of my grad students told me he was planning to spend the summer at Caracol, I asked him to check out this place. He brought back a polaroid of those jaguar figures I showed you this afternoon. And I knew someone had made a big mistake."

Jane was still thinking about the logger. "It was lucky, for the villagers I mean, that the logging operation went bust when it did, just a mile from the site."

"Luck? I'm not sure I believe in luck." Cleis's long hands hung loosely between her knees. "Look into Ixbalum's face and tell me you still believe it was just bad luck that the skidders kept breaking down, that the bridges collapsed, that every worker who didn't get bitten by a fer-de-lance ran off in ones and twos babbling about the jungle cat that was out to get them."

Jane remembered driving along the logging track, her feeling that the jungle was breathing on the back of her neck, stalking her like a big cat.

Jane listened to the steady, still-awake breathing of Cleis in the other bunk. She could see the next few weeks unrolling before her like sticky fly paper, the jungle whispering to her *Let go, let go, there's no one here to care*, but if she let go now, if she let her armor slip just once, the damage would be permanent: she would have been seen, known. Cleis was always there.

Jane turned on her side, careful not to make any noise or disturb the sheet that was pulled up to her shoulders. She thought about Cleis's toffee-colored eyes, the way they watched her all the time. What did they see?

At mid-afternoon the sun was still strong and heat wrapped around Jane like a thick tongue. A hundred yards away, the waterfall roared, tossing spray into the already humid air. The light was perfect: green-gold and viscous as honey, seeping into every crevice and old chisel cut, easing out details ordinarily invisible. With luck, she would be able to photograph this whole section while the light lasted. She set up her specially adapted tripod and tilted the camera up to the next section of curtain wall. More jaguars, more pictures of the plant that Cleis did not recognize.

"I just don't know what it is," Cleis had said the night before, and pulled out four polaroids she had taken days before. "And it's depicted exactly the same in each glyph, always bent with these six fronds facing outward to show the spider web veins. That's significant. It suggests ritual function. And it's always in conjunction with these glyphs here." She tilted the pictures towards the feeble light of the Coleman lamp streaming through their doorway, so that Jane could see.

"Jaguars and women?"

"Jaguars, yes, but they're not portrayed symbolically. It's almost as if they're ... pets or something." She sighed and rubbed her eyes. "And these women are all young. You can tell by their clothes." Jane took Cleis's word for it. "If I didn't know better, I'd say these glyphs represented some kind of purdah, spent behind the curtain walls. Though what that has to do with the jaguars I don't know. And then there are these damned plants.... It's so frustrating! If only these people would talk to me!"

Jane looked at the photos again, tapped two glyphs of women covered in what looked like blood. "What does this mean? Some kind of execution?"

"No. Look at them carefully. Both are wounds to the left shoulder, on the muscle: ritual again."

"Scarification?"

"I don't know what the hell it is. I feel as though I should understand what all this means, but it's just out of my reach."

Jane touched the limestone carvings, weathered now, and tried to imagine the glyphs fresh and new. The carver had squatted out here in the ninety degree heat with only soft bronze tools and pieces of dirty string to make sure everything was straight. A labor of months. Years. It was terrible to think that all that effort—the sweat and bruised palms, the pads of fingers callused and permanently white with limestone dust—now meant nothing because no one knew what these enigmatic, bulbous figures represented.

The camera whirred, clicked, whirred again. Jane, stiff after squatting so long, stood and stretched. Froze. Behind her, arms folded, face dappled with tree shadow, stood Ixbalum.

They looked at each other. Jane could not speak Mopan Maya. She lifted a hand in greeting. Ixbalum stared back impassively. Jane cleared her throat. It sounded impossibly loud. She wondered how long Ixbalum had been watching her. "I have to take these pictures," she said, pointing at her camera. "The light won't last forever."

Ixbalum did not move.

Jane cleared her throat again. She hesitated, then wiped the sweat from her face and doggedly tilted the camera to a different angle. She had a job to do.

Ixbalum's gaze settled on the back of her neck, as hot as the sun. She bent to the viewfinder, focused carefully on a jaguar figure.

She straightened abruptly, turned to Ixbalum.

"Tell me what it means," she said, pointing at the glyphs. "They're your people, Ixbalum. Don't you want the world to hear what they had to say?"

Ixbalum might as well have been carved from the same stone as the glyphs, but the breeze in the trees stirred and the leaf shadow on the Mayan woman's face shifted. Her eyes were yellow, like hammered gold.

Jane stepped back, bumped into her tripod, had to turn quickly to catch it. When she turned back, Ixbalum was gone.

Later, when the sun was slipping behind the trees and the light was more green than gold, when Jane was treading carefully along the trail, camera slung over one shoulder, tripod on the other, she felt that same heat on the back of her neck, as though she was being watched. She stopped, turned slowly. Nothing.

Ten yards further down, she felt it again. This time she put down her camera, dropped her tripod into her other hand to hold it like a club, and turned.

Six feet away, inside her own bootprint, was a jaguar track so fresh that a piece of dirt tottering on the edge of one of the toe marks fell into the depression as she watched.

"Jaguar? You're sure?" Cleis was sitting cross-legged on her bunk, surrounded by notes.

"It looked like cat to me." Jane leaned her tripod in the corner, began to sort automatically through her film stock. "And the print must have been four or five inches across."

"Ocelot, margay?"

"I didn't think they got that big."

"You heard nothing?"

"Not a thing." Fear made her sound angry. If she had not remembered so clearly touching the spoor with her fingertip, then retrieving her camera, taking a picture, she might be tempted to assume she had imagined the incident. But it was real. A jaguar, a predator, had been a few feet behind her, and she had not known it.

Cleis set aside her notes, rubbed her eyes. "The light's terrible in here." Jane remembered the hot gold of Ixbalum's eyes, and shivered. Cleis studied her. "Did you know that 'jaguar' comes from a South American word, yaguara, that means 'wild beast that kills its prey in one bound'? They have very short, powerful limbs and the strength of their jaws is incredible. Pound for pound, they have the most powerful bite of any land-based predator. When I was in the Xingu Basin two or three years ago, I saw a tapir that had been killed by a jaguar: the back of its skull was sheared clean off."

All Jane could think of was Ixbalum's short, squat legs, the muscles along her jaw.

"As far as I know, there has only ever been one reported case of a jaguar attacking people: and that was thirty years ago in Guatemala." Cleis, Jane realized, knew she was scared, and was giving her information to deal with because it would help. She was being humored. "Apparently, four men were killed at a convent."

Despite herself, Jane was intrigued. "A convent?"

Cleis grinned. "They probably did something very unchristian to one of the novices and the other nuns banded together and hacked the men to death with machetes, scythes, garden shears. No local doctor is going to argue cause of death with good sisters, especially when the church probably controls the medical supplies and the hospital." She glanced at her notes, then back to Jane. "Anyway, my point is that jaguars simply don't attack people. Why should they? There's too much to eat around here as it is. Maybe it was following you because you smelled interesting. Maybe it was an adolescent, practicing."

67

Maybe it was trying to intimidate me. But that was ridiculous.

The humidity was thick enough to stand on and the sky was low and gray. Cleis threw her knapsack into the jeep, climbed behind the wheel. "I'll stay overnight in Benque Viejo," she said. "I've a few things to do."

Jane glanced at the sky. "Think it'll rain?"

Cleis shook her head. "It can't. I can't afford it to."

Jane's clothes were already stuck to her. "Don't forget the beer."

"I won't."

Later, alone on the trail to Kuchil Balum, Jane felt as though she were walking through another world: there was no breeze, and every sound, every smell was singular and intense.

The air under the trees grew hotter and more damp.

Jane stumbled over a hidden tree limb. She fell to one knee, her nose seven inches from a log over which Azteca ants marched in an endless, silent line. And it was as if she had been looking at the world through a camera and had only just found the right focus. Everywhere she looked life leapt out at her: huge black carpenter bees buzzing around red melastoma flowers the size of roses; a leaf-frog, gaudy and red-eyed, peering from the depths of a sapodilla; the flicker of a gecko's tail. And there were millipedes and rove beetles, silverfish and woodlice, and spiders spinning their silent webs to catch them. The air was luxuriant with rot, like the breath of a carnivore.

She stood up feeling hot and hunted and hemmed in. A snake slithered in the undergrowth. Her heart began to thump like a kettle drum. She licked salt from her lips, wondered how many different eyes were watching her from behind tree trunks or under leaves. A twig snapped under a heavy paw. Something big was coming towards her … *yaguara, a South American word meaning "predator that kills its prey in one bound."* She ran.

Night seeped through the trees like tea and gathered under her bunk. She sat on the rough blanket fully clothed, facing the door. A shelf bracket pressed into her shoulder blade but she stayed where she was. The jungle was full of eyes.

She dozed and dreamed she was walking to the ruins in thin moonlight. Sliding earth and metal sounds came from the direction of the purdah house. Cleis was digging feverishly, lips skinned back with the effort, teeth glinting like old bone. "It's here somewhere," she was muttering to herself, "I just have to keep digging." Jane wanted her to stop, just for a moment, but she could not seem to get close enough to touch Cleis. She would walk towards her and stretch out her hand only to find that she had gone the wrong way and Cleis was behind her. Then suddenly Cleis was laughing. "Yes!" she shouted, and threw away the shovel, and she was digging with her hands, throwing the dirt back between her legs like a cat. "I've found it!" She looked up at Jane, and her eyes were golden, and suddenly the dirt was piling up around Jane, burying her, and she could not breathe—

Jane surged off the bunk, swallowing, and staggered outside. The night was silent, the four-in-the-morning lull before dawn.

The jeep bumped into the clearing a little after midday. Jane ran to greet Cleis.

"Well, hello to you too," Cleis said. "What have I done to deserve this honor?"

Jane stopped abruptly. "Did you bring the beer?"

Cleis nodded. "I would have driven faster if I'd known you were so desperate. Give me a hand unloading this stuff."

They lugged the new gas bottles inside. Cleis pulled the cardboard off a six-pack and submerged the bottles in the galvanized pail. "Should cool off quickly." She trundled an empty gas bottle out of the way for Jane. "You get some good pictures yesterday?"

"Yes."

"Any rain?"

"No."

They unloaded foodstuff for a while in silence. "According to Radio Belize, the rains will be late this year."

"That's good."

"I see you've lost none of your talent for conversation." Cleis sighed. "Sorry. That was uncalled for. It's just that I've got things on my mind and I wanted…" She shook her head. "Doesn't matter."

Jane watched Cleis slide the orange tubing into place on the gas bottle, turn the knob on the stove, listen for the hiss. She looked different. Something had happened in Benque Viejo.

Cleis opened a beer. "Let's go up to the site. It's cool by the water."

They took the pail and an extra six-pack up the trail and sat on the grassy bank together. Cleis threw stones, opened her second beer, sucked half down without pausing. They listened to the waterfall.

Cleis popped open her third bottle, seemed to come back from wherever she had been. "So, how was your night alone in the jungle?"

Jane wondered if Cleis knew she had been terrified. "I was … Well, I felt skittish, had bad dreams."

Cleis nodded. The sun glinted on tiny beads of sweat on her upper lip. "It was like that for me the time I spent four months in the Xingu basin in Brazil. Years ago. Strange place, the jungle. Feels alive sometimes, and then other times...you wonder what the hell you were worried about."

Jane started on the second six-pack about mid-afternoon. Despite the weight of the heat, she felt lighter than she had done in a long time.

"How come your first name's Cleis?" she asked. She was sitting next to Cleis who was sprawled out on the turf, hair almost touching Jane's thigh. Jane wondered idly what that hair would feel like wrapped around her fingers.

"My mother was fond of poetry. Read lots of the classics in Colombia, when she was young. Don't look so surprised."

"I'm not surprised."

Cleis did not seem to hear her. "She may have ended up in poverty in East LA, and I might have had to do everything on scholarship, be twice as good as the Anglos to get what I wanted, but we have a history, a past. America isn't the only place where people know things."

"Cleis was Sappho's daughter." *Now why did I say that?*

"I know."

A kingfisher flashed blue and green and black across the pool. "Get kingfishers in England," Jane said.

"I know that too." Cleis climbed to her feet. "Time for a swim." She pulled off her shirt, unzipped her shorts. "Aren't you coming in?"

Fear squeezed Jane's throat. "I'm not sure it's wise to swim after so much to drink."

"Three beers? Besides, look at this place!"

The pool was green and quiet. Damsel flies hummed over the surface at the edge away from the fall where water cabbage floated, leaves like huge furry clams. Along the northern bank heliconias with leaves as big as canoe paddles made a dense wall between the forest and water on one side. No one would see.

Jane shook her head. "No. I can't swim."

"Well you could just paddle a bit." Cleis's body gleamed like polished hardwood. "The floor slopes gently. No danger of falling into a pit. And I'm here."

I know. "I'd rather not."

"The water's cool."

Jane was aware of sweat running over her stomach, trickling down the small of her back, itching behind her knees. Swimming would be lovely. She almost moved. Almost stood up and took off her shirt, but years of habit and training brought her up short just as effectively as a chain around her neck. "No." It came out flat and hard.

Cleis's eyes narrowed. "What is it? You don't think a bare-assed Latina is good enough to swim with?"

"It's not that."

Cleis stood with her hands on her hips. "What then?"

Jane drained the bottle of its last, warm mouthful. *Armored, inviolate, safe.* "You wouldn't understand." Immediately, she knew she had said the wrong thing.

"So. Now I'm stupid as well as inferior. What is your problem, Lady Jane? You drive in here, cool as cut glass, and act like you're queen of the fucking world. You smile at me so politely and ask me questions for your damn article. You take my picture, you listen to me rambling on, but you give me nothing. Not one thing. Why? Because deep down you think you're better than me. Better than everyone."

"No. That's not it. It's just that …"

Cleis lifted her eyebrows, waiting, and Jane realized that she was being goaded. For once, she allowed it.

"Why is everyone so eager to show everything to everyone all the time? Everywhere you look there are people being stared at: television, film, video, magazines, newspapers. Close-ups taken from a mile away, such huge scale that pores look like craters. You can't hide anything. Everyone looking, being looked at. Gossip columnists. Stalkers. Tell-all biographies. Desperate actors having their faces sculpted to look like last week's star. It never stops." She was panting.

"What exactly are you afraid of?"

Jane blinked. "What do you mean, what am I afraid of? Those people are being eaten alive! Everything they do or say is consumed by a greedy public. A woman's child is mown down on the street and the cameras are there: tracking her tears, recording the snot on her chin, following the way she shifts from foot to foot because she needs the bathroom. Sometimes they follow her *into* the bathroom. Once you start giving them something, once they see the hairline crack in your armor, they're there, driving in, wedging you open, spilling your guts."

"I still don't understand why it bothers you so much." Jane stared at her. "Look, suppose they wired up your bathroom and made a tape of you taking a dump, complete with groanings and strainings, so what? So fucking what. It's something every person on this earth does. Nothing to be ashamed of."

"But it's private! It's my life...."

"You don't have a life. You're so afraid someone will take it away you haven't allowed yourself one."

"No! That's not—"

"Then why are you so scared?"

Cleis gestured at her own nakedness, at Jane in her hot, itchy clothes, the cool lake, the empty jungle. All of a sudden, horrifyingly, Jane did not know why. She was twenty-nine years old and had spent her whole life hiding behind a mask, and she did not know why. She had denied herself so much: never had a lover, never been naked in public, never been drunk or screamed out loud with pleasure except in the privacy of her own apartments. She had never had a friend, never had a real argument, never wept over a dead pet.

She looked blindly out over the water. Normal people swam naked and did not care. She was not normal. She did not know what she was, or who. She wanted to lay her head down on the turf and cry: grieve for all those lost years. But even now the habit of privacy was too strong.

"It's never too late to change," Cleis said. And she waded out into the pool and dived underwater.

Jane watched the ripples. She knew she could not swim naked in that pool. Not today. But she could, at least, get drunk.

The sun was sinking when she woke. She sat up, and her head thumped. There were mosquito bites on her legs and one already swelling on her left breast. She looked around. Cleis's clothes were gone.

She knelt down and splashed her face with water, trying to think. Beer bottles clinked. She gathered them up, then felt foolish and put them down; counted them. Twelve. And Cleis had had three, four at most. She swayed and realized that she was still drunk. But she never got drunk.

"Cleis!" She climbed carefully up the western slope to the purdah house. "Cleis!" She listened, walked south towards the glyph-covered walls, stopped. She heard something, a vague scrabbling coming from the tumbled remains of a masonry wall.

Cleis was half-lying, half-sitting against a stack of newly fallen stone. Her left arm hung useless and bloody. She was swearing, very quietly, and trying to push herself upright.

"Cleis?"

Cleis smiled lopsidedly. "Fucking thing." She sounded cheerful. Shock, Jane decided.

Jane peered at her eyes. They were glassy. "Do you hurt anywhere except your shoulder?"

"Shoulder?" Cleis looked at it. "Oh."

"Yes. Do you hurt anywhere else? Did you fall, bang your head?" Cleis's left arm was broken by the looks of it, and the gashes on her shoulder would need stitches.

There was no sign of a head injury, but you could not be too careful.

"…fucking thing knocked the wall down on purpose. Kill that fucking thing.…"

It was getting dark. She needed to get Cleis to a safe place. First she needed to make a sling.

She touched the buttons of her shirt, hesitated. *Does it matter?* Oh yes, it still mattered. But there was no real choice. She shivered, despite the heat, then wrenched it off, trying not to imagine a grainy telephoto image of her breasts appearing on newsstands around the country. She draped the shirt around Cleis's neck, tied the sleeves together. "Help me, damn it." But Cleis was lost in a world of shock and pain. Jane thrust the arm into the support.

Later, Jane never really knew how she managed to get them both back down the trail safely. She manhandled Cleis out of the rubble and laid her on the smooth grass. Cleis was too heavy to carry far, Jane could not drag her by the arms.… She took off her belt, slid the leather tongue under the small of Cleis's back, under and around Cleis's belt, then threaded it through the buckle. Tugged. It should hold.

The forest was hot and close. The light was going rapidly. Jane plodded along, dragging Cleis behind her like a sled.

Two thirds of the way down the trail, Ixbalum was there, standing in the leaf shadow, eyes invisible. *Eyes. Cameras. Don't think about it.* "Help me." She did not know if Ixbalum understood or, if she did, whether she cared. "Please."

Ixbalum turned and said something over her shoulder. Two men with the same sloping foreheads and close together eyes of figures depicted in thousand year old glyphs stepped from behind her.

"Be careful," Jane said, half to Ixbalum, half to the men. "Her arm's broken."

Ixbalum gestured for Jane to move aside. Jane stayed where she was. If she could just keep hold of the belt that connected her to Cleis she would not feel naked. "She might have hurt her head, too." The men stepped around her. One gently pried the belt from Jane's hand.

"It was a jaguar," Cleis suddenly said, very clearly.

"What—" But they were picking Cleis up and Jane had to scramble to follow them down the trail.

The tallow candle flickered and sent shadows dancing over Cleis's sleeping face. On her chair by the bed, Jane huddled deeper into the coarse cotton wrap that Ixbalum had held out to her without comment, and tried to stay awake. She felt feverish with too much sun and alcohol and fatigue, and she wondered when Ixbalum would be back.

Cleis opened her eyes. "This isn't our shack."

"You're in Ixbalum's house. How do you feel?"

"I don't know yet. Confused. What happened?"

"A wall fell on you. About eight hours ago. Don't move your arm. It's splinted."

"Broken?" Jane nodded. Cleis closed her eyes. Opened them. "Help me sit up." She hissed with pain when Jane lifted her. "Feel like I've been run over by a truck." She wrinkled her nose. "What's that terrible smell?"

"Some salve or other Ixbalum put on your shoulder. You have some bad cuts."

"On my left shoulder?" She seemed tense. Jane nodded. That answer did not seem to please her. "Anything else?"

"Just bruises."

"Where?"

"Legs, mainly."

"No ... blood?"

"Except from your arm, no."

"You're sure?"

"I'm sure."

Tears ran, sudden and silent, down Cleis's cheeks. Jane looked around; there was nothing in Ixbalum's hut that might do as a tissue.

"You're all right." Jane realized she had never had to reassure anyone before; there had always been someone else, someone closer to do the comforting. "Really. No head injury. And your arm should be fine in a few—"

"I'm pregnant."

Jane did not have the faintest idea how to respond.

"I found out for certain in Benque Viejo. Just over three months gone." Jane got up, dipped her a bowl of water from the barrel by the door. "Thank you." She looked up, met Jane's eyes. "Aren't you going to ask me if it's good news?"

Cleis seemed thin and vulnerable, her eyes big, and Jane wished she knew how to comfort her. "Is it?"

Cleis nodded. "I'm forty-one. I've never loved anyone enough to have a child with them. Last year I realized I probably never would. So I decided to have one on my own. It took me ten months of trying. I thought that wall coming down...." She was crying again. This time Jane wiped away the tears with her hands.

"You're all right. You're all right."

"I'm sorry." And Jane thought she might be apologizing for more than the tears.

After a while, Cleis looked around at the smooth adobe walls, the herbs hanging from the roof. "Where's Ixbalum?"

"She went out about two hours ago." They had not exchanged a single word. Jane had just watched while the Mayan woman washed Cleis's wounds, slathered them with an already prepared salve, bound them. When Ixbalum had gestured for her to help with the split-branch splints, she had.

"I want to get out of here."

So did Jane. She never wanted to see Ixbalum and those golden eyes that had seen her naked again.

Cleis pushed aside the glass of water and the pills that Jane was holding out. "I don't want them. Not yet. I don't know what's going on, but I don't like it." She was flushed, sweaty. Jane wondered if she had made a mistake encouraging Cleis to walk back to their shack so soon. At least she was lying down now.

"Take the pills. You have a fever, and your arm must hurt."

"Of course it hurts. Christ knows what crap she put on it. How do I know my arms's not rotting off?"

They had already been through this. "I watched her wash it. She seemed to know what she was doing." She should have come here and got the first aid kit, proper antiseptics, antibiotic creams, but she had been too drunk, too shaken up from the conversation by the pool. And Ixbalum had been so ... competent. She said, again, "I don't know what the salve was but it was fresh—moist, green-smelling—and the bowl looked clean."

"But why was it fresh? How did she know I'd need it?" Cleis was getting more and more fretful.

"Just take these pills. Everything will seem better when you've had some sleep."

Cleis plucked for a moment at the blanket. "Oh, give me the god damn things then." She swallowed them. "Now will you listen to me?"

Jane sighed. "Go ahead."

"I was looking at the glyph wall, wondering what was under all those vines, thinking maybe I should start clearing them away the next day, when it suddenly struck me how, I don't know, how orderly the vines seemed. So I squatted down and had a closer look: they were growing from the dirt an even eight inches apart. They'd been cultivated. To hide the glyphs. I stood up, thinking maybe I'd tug on them a bit, see how—"

"No wonder the wall came down!" Jane's voice was loud with relief, and it was then that she realized how scared she was.

"But I didn't actually pull on them. I was just thinking about it."

"You'd been drinking. We both had. All that beer..." *Go to sleep,* she was thinking. *I don't want to hear this.*

"I didn't touch that damn wall. The jaguar did it."

Jane closed her eyes. Those dreams of danger and golden eyes.

"Did my face look like that when you were telling me about the jaguar that followed you home from the ruins?" Cleis reached out, grasped Jane's wrist. Her hands felt thinner, dry. "Listen to me, Jane. Just listen. Don't think, not yet. A jaguar knocked down that wall, wounding my shoulder, my left shoulder, like those young women in the glyphs. Ixbalum knew we were coming, and that I was hurt. She had to know, there's no other explanation for the salve and her appearance on the trail. How much do you bet that some of those herbs hanging upside down from her roof are the same as the plants pictured on the glyph wall?"

No, Jane thought, and felt the same fear as that day when she had turned around and seen a jaguar print crumbling inside her own footprint. "You're feverish," she said firmly. "Maybe there was a jaguar, yes. Maybe the ruins have become the stamping grounds of some solitary cat. But that doesn't alter the fact that you need to get to sleep. Now. You need to get some rest and get well."

Cleis was pale now, her lids drooping. "You believe me, I know you do. Because you're scared. I'm scared." Her chin was sinking onto her chest now, eyes barely open. "Ritual wounding... How did she know?" Her eyes closed. "Fucking thing. You'll see...."

Jane sat where she was for more than half an hour, watching Cleis sleep, telling herself that Cleis was wrong.

Jane half-woke in the middle of the night. Her muscles were relaxed, soft; she felt content. Across the room moonlight showed a tangle of blankets pushed back from an empty bed. There was some reason why she should be disturbed by that, but she was already falling back to sleep.

The next time she woke moonlight and shadow patterns had moved further along the wall, and Cleis's bed was no longer empty. She crept out of bed, padded over to the other bunk. She must have dreamed that Cleis was gone, earlier. Cleis was sleeping soundly, naked as usual. Jane checked to make sure no blood was seeping through the bandages, then simply watched her for a while.

Cleis woke late the next morning. Jane brought her water and fruit, checked her fever. "Not as bad as yesterday, but still too high for you to be out of bed."

Cleis twisted restlessly under her blanket. "You should be out working. Just because I have to spend the damn day in bed wasting precious time doesn't mean the rains are going to come later than planned."

"Your color's better," Jane said.

"Well I hurt. My legs, my shoulders … strange places. All my tendons feel pulled."

"You'd better take some more painkillers."

"I don't want any more drugs." She touched her stomach. "Anyway, they give me strange dreams. I feel exhausted from running around the jungle in my dreams." She looked up at Jane crossly. "*Now* what's the matter? I'm fine. I'll take the damn pills. Go do some work."

Work, at least, would mean she would not have to think.

"And before you go, hand me those notes. I can be of *some* use." Jane picked up the nearest camera case, opened the door. "And Jane, I think I was a bit delirious last night. Said some wild things. Just forget it, okay?"

Jane nodded mutely.

Cleis's fever lasted three days. She was up and about before then. "Don't tell me I should rest. I'm fine. Never better. I don't need two good arms to study the glyphs. And the rains won't wait."

The first couple of days at the site, Jane kept a surreptitious eye on Cleis, but gave up when Cleis caught her at it and glared. They worked in silence, Jane moving crabwise with camera and tripod along walls, changing filters, checking light levels; Cleis making notes, taking measurements, staring blankly at the trees and muttering to herself.

On the fourth day, Jane got back to the shack to find Cleis sitting on the bed with her notes, and the remains of the splint piled in a heap on the table. "I took it off," Cleis said. "My arm feels fine. It was probably just a sprain."

There was nothing Jane could say. She cleared away the mess.

Something had changed since Cleis's accident: children now ran past their shack, playing games, and more than once Jane had seen villagers walking through the trees to the their milpas, mattocks on their shoulders. They had greeted her with a smile and a wave.

Sometimes, too, she would look up from her camera to see Cleis and Ixbalum together, out of earshot, talking. Jane wondered why Ixbalum was now willing to speak to Cleis; wondered what she was saying, what craziness she was spilling into Cleis's eager ears. But she did not ask. Instead, she tried to push Cleis from her mind by working from first light until last. At night she would lie down, exhausted, and fall into troubled sleep. Her dreams were vivid and fractured. More than once she woke to find Cleis gone from her bed. *Where do you go?* Jane wanted to ask, *and how?* But she never did. She imagined Cleis and Ixbalum gliding through the jungle, looking into the dark with their golden eyes....

One night her dreams were jumbled images: time running backwards while she watched the ruins reform into a city; vast storms overhead; Cleis talking to her earnestly, explaining. "Ixbalum doesn't care what I know anymore. It doesn't matter what the children tell me. I'm hers now." Jane woke drenched in sweat. She looked over at Cleis's bed: she was sleeping like a baby.

Am I going mad?

She needed to get away. She got out of bed, pulled on her clothes.

She waited until just after dawn to wake Cleis. "The photography is ahead of schedule, and we need supplies. I'm driving to Benque Viejo. I'll be gone two or three days."

Jane had expected to reach Benque Viejo, walk through its streets, loud with traffic and thick with the stink of leaded gasoline, and come slowly out of her nightmare. All the time she was pulling Belize dollars from her wallet for bottled gas and beer and canned food she wondered when it would stop feeling strange and dangerous to be back in the world.

She booked herself into a hotel and took a bath, but the water was only lukewarm and she found herself longing for the lake with its water cabbage and kingfisher.

After weeks of eating fish and fruit and corn, the steak dinner was alien and almost inedible. She left a tip on the table and walked from the restaurant into the street. The sky was dusky pink, streaked with pearl gray clouds. She wished Cleis could be there to see it. And then she knew she did not want to spend three days here in Benque Viejo when she could be at Kuchil Balum. The rains would be coming soon. There was no time. Because when the rains came, Cleis would go back to New Mexico, and she….

What is happening to me? She did not know. All she knew was that she had to get back.

It was mid-afternoon of the next day when she parked in front of their shack. Cleis was not there. *Probably at the site. No matter.* Jane took her time unloading the supplies, nervous about seeing Cleis again.

Then there was nothing left to do; she had even washed the enamel plates that had been lying on the table—the same plates she and Cleis had eaten from the night before she had left for Benque Viejo. She tried not to worry. Cleis had probably been eating straight from a can, too busy to take the time to prepare anything. She checked the shack one last time, then set off for the ruins.

The waterfall fell peacefully, a flock of black and orange orioles wheeled about the crown of a tree at the edge of the clearing, but there was no Cleis.

"Cleis!" The call echoed back, and Jane remembered the last time she had called to Cleis here. Had something else happened, something worse?

She ran through the ruins, calling, ducking in and out of half-excavated buildings. Nothing. Maybe she was at the village, talking to Ixbalum.

Two women stood at the well, a man plucked a chicken on his doorstep. They looked up when Jane ran into the clearing. "Cleis?" she asked. They frowned. "Cleis?" she asked again, pantomiming curls falling from her head. "Ah," they said, and shook their heads.

Jane ran to Ixbalum's hut. The door was closed. She banged on it with her fist. No reply. She banged again, then pushed her way in.

Without the candles, the hut was cool and dark. There was no one there. Jane brushed aside bunches of herbs on her way back to the door, then turned around again and plucked a leaf from each bundle. She could look at them later, see if any matched the ritual leaf on the glyphs.

She was just putting them in her pocket when Ixbalum came in.

The Mayan woman stood there with her arms folded, looking at Jane, looking at the floor where one leaf lay in the dirt. Jane picked it up and put it in her pocket with the others. This woman had already seen her naked, and drunk, and she was too concerned for Cleis to feel any shame at being found in Ixbalum's hut. "I want to know where Cleis is."

Ixbalum said nothing. Jane could feel herself being studied. This time she did not cringe.

"If you know where she is, I want to know. She's pregnant, and I think that fall was more of a shock than she knows. I want to take her away from here." *I do?* "I'm asking for your help."

Ixbalum moved so suddenly that Jane thought she was going to strike her, but Ixbalum reached up past Jane's left ear and drew a leaf from one of the bunches. She held it out to Jane.

"I don't understand." But she did.

Ixbalum shook the leaf in front of Jane's face. The message was unmistakable: Take it. Jane did. Ixbalum nodded, very slightly, then made a *Go now* gesture and turned her back.

Not knowing what else to do, knowing only that it was pointless shouting when neither understood the other, Jane went back out into the sunshine. The leaf was a big one, dull grey-green now, but it would have been bright when fresh, the color of the paste Ixbalum had smeared on Cleis's shoulder. It had six points, and a tracery of veins like a spider's web.

Night came as a rising cloud of living sound. The creaky chorus of thousand of insects rubbing together chitinous legs and wing combs echoed and reverberated through the trees. Fireflies streaked the dark with yellow.

Jane lay on her back on her bunk. Her arms were grazed and scratched from pushing aside branches, being caught by unexpected thorns. She had cut her palm on a frond of razor grass. Her throat was sore from calling. For the first time she was unclothed and not covered with a sheet. She lay naked to the world, as an offering. *Please come back. Just come back safe.*

Cleis returned at dusk the next day. She pushed the door open and walked in slowly. Her hair was filthy, her face drawn. She stopped when she saw Jane. "You're back early." Her voice was flat with exhaustion.

Jane wanted to touch her face, hold her, make sure she was all right. "I got back yesterday. I've been waiting, and worrying. I went out looking." Cleis swayed a little. "It's dangerous to get too tired out there."

Cleis sat down on her bunk, sighed and closed her eyes as she leaned back against the wall. "I didn't know you'd be here to worry."

"I just…" Jane did not know how to explain why she had come back early. "I just wanted to know where you've been."

Cleis's eyes flicked open. Underneath, her skin was dark with fatigue, but the eyes themselves were bright, intense. "Do you? Do you really?"

Jane took a deep breath; she felt very vulnerable. "Yes."

"The simple answer," Cleis said, over a cup of hot tea, "is that I don't know where I've been." They were sitting at the table, a Coleman lamp drawing moths that fluttered against the screen. Jane had insisted that Cleis eat something, rest a little, before talking. "The complex answer… What do you know about dreaming?"

Jane was momentarily thrown off balance. "Not much."

"Dreams are something I researched in my twenties, a long time before becoming interested in Mayan civilization. Simply stated, the human brain exists in three parts, one cobbled onto the other, communicating uneasily, each with different… behaviors. There's the first evolutionary stage, the reptile or R-complex, the crocodile brain whose realm is sexual, aggressive, and ritual behavior. Then when mammals evolved from reptiles, they developed the limbic system, which meant they perceived the world differently—in terms of signs, and vivid sensory and emotional images. To do this, they had to bypass the crocodile brain, suppress it. They couldn't ignore it altogether, though, because it controlled a lot of the body's physical functions: the urge to fuck and fight and eat."

"What does all this have to do with where you were last night?"

"I'm getting there. Anyway, mammals found a way to turn the R-complex, the crocodile brain back on, harmlessly, during sleep. Which means, of course, that our dreams are the crocodile's dreams: sex and food and fighting." Her eyes were bright. "Haven't you ever wondered why we get clitoral erections during dreams?"

"No."

"Then some mammals developed the neocortex. We became self conscious. Ever wondered why you can't read or do math in your dreams?"

Jane opened her mouth to say she had never noticed whether or not she could, then remembered countless dreams of opening books only to be frustrated by meaningless squiggles.

Cleis noticed and nodded. "The neocortex handles analytic recollections. It's usually turned off when we dream. That's why dreams are so hard to remember. When I change, I become a mammal with no neocortex. My waking state is like a dream state. When I change back, when I "wake," I remember very little. So, in answer to your question: I don't know where I've been."

There was a bubble of unreality around Jane's head, around the whole room. She concentrated on her hands, neatly folded together before her on the table. *My hands are real.* "What are you trying to tell me?"

Cleis reached out and touched those neatly folded hands. "I think you already know."

Jane felt very calm. She pulled the six-fronded leaf from her pocket. "You believe in this."

Cleis said nothing.

"You think... You think that those glyphs on the purdah wall are true. That the ritual wounding has purpose." She remembered Ixbalum shaking the leaf in her face. "You think your accident wasn't an accident. That Ixbalum infected you with some kind of, I don't know, changing agent, a catalyst. That you can become... that you change into a jaguar."

Now laugh. Tell me it isn't true. But Cleis just nodded. "Yes."

"Do you know how that sounds?" Her voice was very even, but her heart felt as though it was swelling: so big it was pushing at her stomach, making her feel ill.

"You've seen the evidence with your own eyes—"

"I've seen nothing! A wall, some pictures, some leaves. You got drunk, pulled the wall on top of you, broke your arm and probably took a bang on the head. Ixbalum fixed you up. You disappear at night and come back looking like hell, with a pseudo-scientific explanation that basically boils down to this: you can't remember and you're not responsible. All the evidence points not to that fact that you've discovered some mystical Mayan rite, but that something is wrong in your head, and getting worse." She put the leaf down carefully on the table. "Look at it. Look at it hard. It's just a leaf."

"I've read the dates on the stelae, Jane. Kuchil Balum, Place of the Jaguar, was occupied up until the sixteenth century."

"What has that got to do with—"

"Think." Cleis's voice was thin and hard, bright as wire. "The lowland Mayan culture began to die more than a millennium ago: population pressure, some say, and crop failures, but I'm fairly sure it was more to do with a loss of faith. But not here. Here the power of the gods was tangible. Young girls from every family were sent to the purdah house at puberty. They were ritually wounded, infected. Some changed, most did not." She searched Jane's face. "Every family had the opportunity, the chance to join the elite. That welded the community together in ways we can't even begin to comprehend."

A moth fluttered frantically against the window screen.

"But even jaguar gods can't stand against guns and missionaries," Cleis continued. "So they pulled down their beautiful stone buildings and built themselves a village that appears unremarkable. They hid, but they've kept their culture, the only Mayans who have, because they have people like Ixbalum."

They sat for a moment in silence. Jane stood up. "I'll make some more tea."

She busied herself with the kettle and teapot. There had to be a way to get Cleis to see past this delusion; some way she could persuade Cleis to pack her bags and leave with her and have her head X-rayed. She did not know what to say, but she knew it was important to keep the dialogue open, to keep Cleis anchored as much as possible in the real world.

The kettle boiled. Jane brought the pot to the table. "It's not the same without milk," she said.

Cleis smiled faintly. "Being an ignorant American, I don't think it's the same without ice."

She seemed so normal.... Jane asked sharply, "When you change, how do you think it affects your child?"

Cleis looked thoughtful. "I don't know." She leaned forward. Jane could feel Cleis's breath on her face. She wanted to strain across the table, feel that breath hot on her throat, her neck. "You haven't asked me how it feels to change. Don't you want to know?"

Jane did. She wanted to know everything about Cleis. She nodded.

"It's like walking through a dream, but you're never scared, never being chased, because you're the one who's dangerous. I'm not me, I'm ... other."

"Other?"

"Here, now, I have a sense of self, I know who I am. I can use symbols. It's..." She frowned. "It's hard to describe. Look at it this way." She patted the table. "I know this table is made of wood, that wood comes from trees, and that this wood is pine. Underlying all that knowledge is the ability to work in symbols—tree, furniture, wood— the ability to see beyond specifics. When I'm changed, symbols, words ... they become meaningless. Everything is specific. A barba jalote is a barba jalote, and a chechem is a chechem. They're distinct and different things. There's no way to group them together as 'tree.' The world becomes a place of mystery, unknowable, unclassifiable; and understanding is intuitive, not rational."

She toyed absently with the leaf.

"I'm guided by signs: the feel of running water, the smell of brocket deer. The world is unpredictable." She paused, sighed, laid her hands on the table. "I just am," she said simply.

The rainy season was not far off. The days were hotter, more humid, and Jane worked harder than before, because when she was busy she did not have to deal with Cleis, did not have to look at her, think about how her skin might feel, and her hair. She did not have to worry about getting Cleis to a hospital.

The nights were different.

They would sit outside under the silky violet sky, sipping rum, talking about the jungle.

"The jungle is a siren," Cleis said. "It sings to me." Sweat trickled down the underside of her arm. Jane could smell the rich, complex woman smells. "Especially at night. I've started to wonder how it would be during the rains. To pad through the undergrowth and nose at dripping fronds, to smell the muddy fur of a paca running for home and know its little heart is beat beat beating, to almost hear the trees pushing their roots further into the rich mud. And above, the monkey troops will swing from branch to branch, and maybe the fingers of a youngster, not strong enough or quick enough, will slip, and it'll come crashing down, snapping twigs, clutching at leaves, landing on outflung roots, breaking its back. And it'll be frightened. It'll lie there eyes round, nose wet, fur spattered with dirt and moss, maybe bleeding a little, knowing a killer is coming through the forest." Cleis's nostrils flared.

Jane sipped her rum. She could imagine the jaguar snuffing at the night air, great golden eyes half-closed, panting slightly; could taste the thin scent molecules of

blood and fear spreading over her own tongue, the anticipation of the crunch of bone and the sucking of sweet
flesh. She shivered and sipped more rum, always more
rum. When the sun was up and she looked at the world
through a viewfinder she did not need the numbing no-
think of rum, but when there was just her and Cleis and
the forest's night breath, there was nowhere to hide.

And so every night she staggered inside and fell across
her bed in a daze; she tried not to smell the salty sun-
shiny musk of Cleis's skin, the sharp scents of unwashed
hair, tried not to lean towards the soft suck and sigh of
rum fumes across the room. Tried, oh tried so hard, to fall
asleep, to hear nothing, see nothing, feel nothing.

But there would be nights when she heard Cleis sit
up, when she could almost feel the weight of Cleis's gaze
heavy on the sheet Jane kept carefully pulled up to her
chin, no matter how hot she was. On those nights she
kept her eyes shut and her mind closed, and if she woke
in the middle of the night and felt the lack of heat, the
missing cellular hum of another human being, she did not
look at Cleis's bed in case it was empty.

But one night, Jane woke sitting up in bed with her eyes
open after a dream of sliding oh so gently over another
woman, sliding in their mutual sweat, and she saw that
Cleis was gone. *I'm alone*, she thought, and was suddenly
aware of every muscle in her body, plump and hot, of her
thighs sliding together, wet and slippery, of her skin wanting to be bare. *There are no cameras here.* She lay her hand
on her stomach, felt tendons tighten from instep to groin.
And before she could really wake up and realize what
she was doing—tell herself that this was not the same as
being alone in her own room, one she could lock—she
was standing naked before Cleis's empty bed, before the
wooden corner post. It came to mid-thigh, a four-by-four
rounded off at the top and polished. She stroked it with
one hand, her belly with the other. Her pubic hair was a

foot away from the post; a foot, then eight inches, then six. She sank to her knees, rubbed her face on the post, held one breast, then the other. One thick drop of milky juice ran down the inside of her thigh. She pressed her belly to the wood, stood up slowly, feeling the top of the post run down between her breasts, down her stomach, her abdomen, then moved away very slightly, oh so very slowly, so the post skipped a beat then skimmed the tops of her thighs.

"Oh yes," she said, imagining Cleis lying face down in front of her, moonlight on her buttocks. "Oh yes."

She crouched down, crooning, leaning over the post, palms resting on the bunk, feet braced on the cool dirt floor. She began to lower herself.

The door creaked open. Jane froze. Something behind her coughed the tight throaty cough of a jaguar; another drop of milky juice ran down her thigh. The animal behind her rumbled deep in its chest. Jane did not dare turn around. It rumbled again: *Don't stop.* Her vulva was hot and slick and her heart thundered. The cough behind her was closer, tighter, threatening: *Do it now.*

Jane licked her lips, felt the golden eyes traveling up her achilles, her calves, the back of her knees, the tendons in her thighs, the cheeks of her bottom. She dare not turn, and she dare not disobey, nor did she want to.

"Ah," she said softly and laid her cheek on the sheet. *Between Cleis's shoulder blades.* Touched the rumpled blanket above her head. *Cleis's rough curls.* And lowered herself onto the beautifully smooth oh so lovely rounded and rich wood. *The swell and heat of Cleis.* She moved gently. "Oh, I love you." And she felt breath on her own clenching bottom, the close attention of whatever was behind her, and suddenly she knew who, what, was behind her and loved her, it. "Yes, I love you," she said, but it was a gasp as she felt the wood round and slick between her legs slide up and down and her breath caught and "Ah," she said, "ah," and she was grunting, and then she felt a sharp cool pressure against her shoulder where claws unsheathed and rested, possessive, dimpling the skin, and she was pulling herself up and over that wooden corner, *Cleis's soft plump slippery-now cheek*, her face tight with effort, and her breasts flattened on the bed as she thrust and her chin strained forward and the muscles under her skin pumped and relaxed and sweat ran down her legs and the room was full of a rumbling purr. Fur brushed her back and she was pressed into the bed by an enormous weight, a weight with careful claws, and the heat between her and the wood was bubbling up in her bones and "Ah!" she shouted, "ah!" hardly able to breathe, and could not stop, not now not now, and she humped and rocked and grunted until she shuddered and screamed and opened and pushed and came, curling around the bunk *around Cleis* like a fist. Sweat ran from her in rivers; a pulse in her temple thumped.

Claws slid back into their sheaths, the heat and weight withdrew. A throaty rumble: *Don't move*. And then it was gone.

Jane buried her face in the damp sheets that smelled of Cleis, that smelled of her and Cleis, and cried. *I don't know where I've been*, Cleis had said, *when I change back, I remember very little.*

When Jane woke up, Cleis was fast asleep in her bunk.

The mid-morning sun poured like buttermilk over Jane where she knelt on the turf before the glyph wall.

What is happening to me?

She rested her fingertips on the glyphs. "What do you really say?" she whispered.

She was alone. Cleis had gone into the forest that morning, saying she wanted to examine the area for evidence of fruit tree cultivation.

She found herself standing by the fall, staring into the sheeting water, mind empty.

Wake up! she told herself fiercely. *Think. Don't let this just happen to you....* She jumped fully clothed into the water.

She bobbed back to the surface, gasping. It was cold. *Good.* She swam back to the bank, climbed out just long enough to strip off her sodden clothes.

She did not even think about whether or not anyone might be watching.

She dived back in and swam in a fast crawl to the waterfall, let it thunder on her head for a moment; swam again.

This is real, she told herself. *This: sun, water, air. Not dreams, not Cleis's delusions.*

She swam until she was exhausted, then climbed out onto the bank and lay in the sun. She fell asleep.

When she woke, the memory of the dream, the soreness between her legs, was still vivid. She sighed. Her rational mind told her one thing, all the evidence *All my needs* told her another. Which did she want to be real? She did not know.

Her clothes had dried in a wrinkled pile. Jane shook them out one by one and put them back on.

The inside of the shack was hotter than the outside. Cleis had been cooking.

"Here," she said, and handed Jane a tin plate. "Beans and tortillas and fresh corn. Let's eat outside."

Jane wondered where the food had come from, but obeyed silently. Cleis seemed different. Cheerful. Jane wondered if it was anything to do with last night, felt the world spin a little. A dream. It had been a dream.

They sat very close together on the step, arms brushing against each other as they ate. Jane watched the small muscles along Cleis's forearm ripple as she chased beans with her fork, wiped at the juice with her tortilla. Her arms seemed thicker, the muscles more solid than they had been. Jane wondered if that was a result of pregnancy. Women plumped out a little, didn't they? She studied Cleis. Not long ago her muscles had been long and flat, face hollow as though the intensity of her concentration burned away all subcutaneous fat. Her eyes had peered bright from dark hollows. Now she seemed squarer, stronger, more lithe.

"I'd like to take more pictures of you."

"You already have all the pictures you'll need for that article."

Jane had almost forgotten the reason she had come to Belize. She felt as though she had always been here, always eaten from tin plates and drunk rum with Cleis. "I didn't mean that. I mean of you, as you... as your pregnancy develops. I want to document your changes."

Changes. The word hung in the air between them.

"Ow!" A sharp pain shot through Jane's left breast. "Christ!" Another shooting pain jerked her arm sending the tin plate flying, beans spattering on Cleis's shorts. Cleis jumped to her feet. Jane clapped a hand to the fire in her breast.

"Move your hand." All Jane could do was gasp. "Move your hand, Jane. I need to see."

But Jane was scared. She did not know what was happening, was afraid to see. "It hurts!"

"Move your hand." This time Jane let Cleis move her hand away, did not protest as she unbuttoned her shirt. She turned her head away as Cleis sucked in her breath.

"What is it?"

"Botfly. It's eating its way out of your breast."

"Get it out! Get it out!" Jane wanted to rip at her breast, at the thing that was eating her flesh, but Cleis was holding her hands.

"Listen to me. Fasten up your shirt again. It's not big. There won't be any permanent damage, but I have to go get something. Can you do that?"

Jane nodded, thinking Cleis meant to get something from the shack. But Cleis set off down the track that led to the village. "Wait!"

"I won't be long. Be brave, bonita."

Jane sat with her breast cupped in her hand. *Bonita.*

It must have been from that mosquito bite she got the day Cleis had broken her arm. The egg of a botfly had hatched on her skin and burrowed its way down into her breast. Now it was big enough to need food. It would stay in her breast, feeding on her flesh, breathing through the hole it would chew through her skin, until it was large enough to hatch into the botfly. Unless they could get it out. The pain was excruciating.

Bonita.

Cleis returned, slightly out of breath and slick with sweat.

"Chew this." She held out a large dried leaf.

"Where did you get it?" Cleis just looked at her. Ix-balum, of course. "What is it?"

"Tobacco."

"Tobacco? What good will that do? That won't take away the pain!"

"It's not for the pain. Just chew it." Cleis tore off a piece, held it out. Jane took it, reluctantly, put it in her mouth, chewed gingerly.

"Tastes terrible."

"Just chew. Don't swallow. No, chew some more." Cleis put down the rest of the leaf and started to unbutton Jane's shirt again. Jane watched her, saw the way the skin around her eyes was wrinkled in concentration, saw the faint sparkle of perspiration on her lip. Jane imagined those long brown hands wrapped around her breasts. She could feel her color rising. She was afraid that her nipples would harden. She cleared her throat. "How does it look?"

"See for yourself."

Jane, still chewing, looked. There was a hole, no bigger than the knob on her watch, about three inches right of her nipple. So small for so much pain.

Cleis held out her hand. "Spit it out." Jane did, feeling a little self-conscious. Cleis pinched off a tiny clump of soggy pulp and rolled it between the strong fingers of her right hand. "This might hurt." She put her left hand on Jane's breast, one finger on each side of the hole, then spread them slightly, so that the pink under her nails turned white and the larva's breathing hole stretched open. Her fingers were very gentle, very precise. Very human. Cleis plugged the hole neatly with the tobacco. "Very brave, bonita. The nicotine will kill it. Then we'll pull it out with a pin." They watched each other's faces as Cleis began to fasten Jane's shirt again, then hesitated. Cleis's eyes were very dark, and a vein in her throat pulsed.

Jane panicked. "The food was nice. Thank you."

Cleis studied her a moment, then half turned away. "Don't thank me, thank our mysterious benefactor. When I got back this afternoon, I found a little pile of stuff, tortillas, corn, fresh fruit for later, on the doorstep."

Jane closed her eyes against sudden nausea as the real world threatened to come unglued.

Cleis, still not looking at her, did not notice. "They've probably finally figured out we're not burning-eyed fanatics clutching bowdlerized bibles in one hand and McDonald's franchises in the other."

Jane nodded, as though she agreed, but she knew: the food was a gift, to their new god.

Every afternoon when they got back from the site there was something: sometimes fruit, or a plucked chicken; eggs; once a clay pot full of some sticky alcoholic beverage. They drank that on the night Cleis used a pin to pull the plug of tobacco, black now, from Jane's breast, and then teased out the botfly larva. Jane held the pin with the skewered larva over the gas ring until it was ashes. She had bad dreams that night, dreams of being eaten alive by wriggling maggots, but when she woke up, Cleis was there. "You killed it Jane. It's dead."

Most nights, Jane woke up to find Cleis gone. She did not speak of it. *Don't reinforce the madness*, she told herself, but sometimes she wondered whose madness. She felt as though she were being sucked into an increasingly angled world, where the beliefs of Cleis and Ixbalum and the villagers, the evidence of forest and ruin, all made sense, if only she would let go of everything that made her sane. Everything that made her human.

The forest is a siren, Cleis had said, and Jane could hear it singing, day and night.

Cleis was changing, spending more and more time in her own world, content to drowse on the warm, sunlit terraces, or stare off into the distance while Jane worked.

Perhaps it was her pregnancy. Jane did not know much about the process, but Cleis grew visibly more pregnant every day, which she did not think was normal.

"We should take you to Benque Viejo for a check up," she said one afternoon when Cleis was waking from a nap. "You're too big for four months."

Cleis shrugged. "The process is being accelerated. Jaguar gestation is only three months."

For the first time in her life, Jane deliberately broke an expensive piece of equipment: she threw the camera she was using against a rock and did not bother to pick up the pieces.

Now when Jane woke up in the mornings she could taste the damp in the air, a different damp, cold, spelling the end of their time here.

Cleis seemed to smell it too. She became restless, always moving about, standing up two minutes after she sat down. She was eating less and less and barely bothered to listen when Jane told her she should eat, for her own health and her child's. Sometimes Jane would come back from the site and find Cleis staring at something—a pen, the stove—as though it were utterly alien.

Cleis began to stay away for longer stretches: all night, then twenty-four hours.

"Why?" Jane wanted to know. "Why are you doing this?"

"I can't help it. It … Everything is so simple out there. I don't need to worry about always having to be better than everyone else just to stay in place. I smell the green and it's like opium. It makes me forget."

And Jane knew she was losing her.

Four days later, Cleis disappeared.

She did not come home one night, or the next day. One night stretched to two, then a week. Jane thought she would go mad. She searched the jungle by day, left messages on rocks and carved words on trees with a knife. She cooked every night, hoping the smell of food would draw Cleis back.

She still went to the site to take pictures. There were probably a hundred thousand glyphs, some of which would not survive another rainy season. And there was always wildlife to photograph. If she just kept taking pictures, Cleis would come back. She would. They would go back to New Mexico together, and Jane would alternately help Cleis put together her notes and visual evidence, and work on a book of photographs of Belize. Everything would turn out all right. She just had to make sure she had everything done for when Cleis returned, before the rains.

One day, walking through the trees with her camera in search of a purple-throated hummingbird, Jane heard a strange noise. A pattering. Something cold hit her face, then her leg, her shoulder. All around her leaves started to bounce, and the stem of a bromeliad trembled as it filled. The patter became a rush.

Rain.

Rivulets of the stuff began to run down the trunk at her back and the rush became a hiss. There was too much water for the forest to absorb, and within seconds there was a muddy brown stream running past her feet. A leaf floated past, with a spider balanced on it, as though it were a life raft.

One week became two, then three. Jane wandered in the rain, imagining Cleis as a jaguar, drinking from the new pools, licking rain drops from her whiskers. Jane no longer left written messages, only her scent, and still Cleis did not come.

One night, something woke Jane. She sat up, listened: the rain had stopped. She got up, went outside. All around the shack were jaguar tracks pressed into the mud.

"Cleis?" But she whispered, afraid. The windows of her shack were screen, and the door flimsy. There were many jaguars in the forest.

When she woke again in the morning, the rain was thrumming steadily on the tin roof. She sighed, pulled on a long shirt and opened the door to take a look at the world.

There, curled in the mud, naked and still, was Cleis. Jane stood in the open doorway, unable to move, throat tight. Then she ran down the steps and knelt beside her. Cleis's hair was reddish brown with mud and a large scratch stretched over her ribs. She looked nine months pregnant.

"Cleis?" Jane touched her, hesitantly, then jerked back when she felt cold flesh. But Cleis opened her eyes.

Getting her up the steps and into the shack was harder than dragging her down the trail, but Jane managed, eventually. She stripped the covers from Cleis's bunk so they would not get wet, sat her down. "Now you keep still while I put a kettle on."

Cleis sat like a cold soapstone carving while Jane rubbed her down with a towel and talked about the rain, the hot tea she would make, the photographs she had been taking. After a few minutes, Cleis began to tremble. Jane kept rubbing.

"That's right. You're home now. You're safe with me." The trembling became great rolling shudders. Jane wrapped a clean dry towel around her. "You don't have to worry about anything. I'll take care of you." She stroked Cleis's hair. "While you've been gone I've been at the site every day, taking pictures. It's changed with the rains, got more lush." Cleis's eyes were still blank, uncomprehending. "The waterfall used to be so clear but now it's muddy. The other day I saw a turtle sunning itself on the bank...." She talked on and on, about everything and nothing, until she felt a hot tear splash on her shoulder. Then she made the tea, guided Cleis's hand to the cup. Watched until she was sure Cleis would hold the tea without burning herself.

"Good. Now you drink that all up while I put a fresh sheet on this bunk, and then we'll get you tucked in nice and cozy and you can sleep for a while." Cleis watched her while she made the bed. Her eyes were deep sunk, surrounded by grainy brown circles the color of tannin. "There. Everything will look better after some sleep."

In sleep, Cleis looked fragile. Her eyelids were delicate with purples: lavender, indigo, violet. Her face was drawn, leached of color, a kind of dirty tan. She had kicked the sheet down to her waist and Jane could see that her breasts were a different shape.

She would give birth soon.

But that's impossible.

Jane sighed. She no longer knew what was possible and what was not. All that mattered was that Cleis had come back. She stroked the lean hand lying on top of the sheet. The fingernails were filthy now, and ragged, but Jane only saw the way that hand had opened her shirt, weeks ago, had gently moved away her own hand, had made her feel better.

She lifted the hand and kissed it. "Oh, I have missed you." Cleis slept on. "As soon as you're well enough, we'll leave this place."

She got up and started packing.

Cleis slept for nearly ten hours, then woke up long enough to be fed some soup. When the soup was gone, she went back to sleep.

When it got dark, Jane lit all three Coleman lamps, even though the heat was overwhelming. If Cleis woke up in the middle of the night, the first thing she wanted her to see was light. Bright, artificial light. She stood by Cleis's bed, hesitating: the other bunk was covered in open suitcases and piles of clothes. Moving them would wake her. Jane drew back the sheet, fitted herself carefully around the strange mix of bone and muscle and pregnancy that was Cleis, and fell asleep almost instantly.

When she woke up it was still the middle of the night. Cleis was whimpering, burrowing into her neck. "Sshh, sshh. I'm here. What is it?" But then Cleis was clinging to her and crying and Jane was stroking her side, shoulders arms side of breast ribs belly-bulge hip and back, up and down, telling her it was all right, it was all right, and then the heat Jane felt was more than the hiss and spit of Coleman lamps, more than the warmth of a humid Belize night. And Cleis was no longer sobbing on her neck but kissing it, and the arms wrapped so tightly around her were pulling her in, until their mouths were almost close enough to touch, and Jane's arm was under Cleis's neck, supporting her head, and her leg was wrapped over Cleis's and her other hand stroking her breast, her hips, her thighs.

"Kiss me," Cleis said.

Jane expected her lips to be dry and rough, but they were soft as plums.

At first they made love as though they were underwater: coming together too fast, bumping, drifting apart, but then they were moving together, rising towards the surface, a roaring in their ears, and the muscles in arms and thighs and belly were clenched tight as each breathed the other's breath as though it were the only oxygen available.

"Show me I'm real," said Cleis, and slid her palm up to the hot slick between Jane's thighs. "Come in my hand." And Jane did.

They lay in each other's arms, slippery as newborns, while Jane kissed Cleis's forehead, again and again.

"I've packed almost everything," Jane said as they ate breakfast. Cleis was wearing a long shirt. Nothing else would fit her. "We need to get you to a clinic as soon as possible. You look like you're ready to give birth any minute."

Cleis rested a hand on her belly. She nodded but did not say anything.

"I'll check the jeep as soon as we've had breakfast." Jane decided not to mention her worries about the passability of the trail in this wet weather. "Will you be all right for the journey?"

Cleis moved her eyes sideways, lifted her shoulders slightly in a *Who knows?* gesture.

"Well... do you feel well enough at the moment?"

Cleis nodded, then seemed to realize she would have to give more than that. "Everything is very strange for me. Different. Sitting here, talking to you, is like looking through a kaleidoscope. Someone keeps twisting it out of shape, and then I don't know who you are, or who I am, or what we're doing here. Talking is sometimes...difficult."

Jane did not want to ask the next question, because she was scared of the answer. But she had to know. "Do you... Is leaving what you want to do?"

Cleis hesitated, then laid a hand on her belly and nodded. Jane knew she would get no more from her for a while.

They set off at midday. It was cold, and pouring with rain. Jane helped Cleis to the passenger seat, more because of Cleis's mental state than any physical disability. Cleis moved easily, muscles plainly visible beneath her skin. Once she was in the jeep Jane wrapped several shirts around her bare legs.

It was slow going. Twice, Jane had to climb out of the jeep and tuck canvas under rear wheels that could find no traction in mud. But she did not mind the rain or the mud or the cold: she was getting Cleis to safety.

All this time, Cleis sat in her bundle of clothes, silent and distant.

Eight miles down the trail they came across a tree that had fallen across their path. Jane turned off the engine. "Stay here. I'll go take a look."

The trunk was too big to drive over and the undergrowth on either side of the trail was too thick to drive through. Jane walked back to the jeep. "I'm going to try to hack us a path around this thing." She reached under the driver's seat and pulled out the machete. "Just stay here and keep the windows and doors locked." Cleis did not seem to hear her. Jane rolled up both windows and locked the doors, hesitated, then took the car keys. "It might take a while."

Jane hurried, swinging the machete heedlessly through vines and flowers. Her arms were aching and her face itched with spattered sap by the time she had a path cleared.

She hurried back to the jeep. "That should—"

Cleis was gone. A pile of empty clothes lay on the passenger seat.

"No," Jane said quietly, "not now." She would not let the forest have her. "Do you hear me?" she bellowed. "I won't let you have her!"

She crashed through the undergrowth, smashing past branches, pushing through tangles, the machete forgotten. She had no idea how long she trampled through the forest, blinded by grief and rage, but eventually she found herself by a stream, sobbing. She wiped the tears from her eyes. Maybe Cleis was already back at the jeep. Maybe she had just wandered off for a moment then remembered who she was. Yes. She should get back to the jeep.

But the jeep was still empty. Jane sat behind the wheel, staring into the trees until it was dark. Then she switched on the lights and drove back to the shack.

She did not unpack the jeep. For the next five nights she left a Coleman lamp burning on the step, just in case. She barely slept any more, but wandered through the trees, calling. On the sixth night she did not go back to the shack. Perhaps if she stayed out here, lived as Cleis lived, she could understand. Her back itched: her shirt was filthy. She took it off, left it hanging on a branch.

That night she slept curled up on a tree bough, like a jaguar. Like Cleis. She woke hours later, heart kicking under her ribs. Did jaguars dream of falling?

The next day she wandered aimlessly through the forest, eating fruit where she found it. She ran her hand across the surface of a puddle, wondered what it would be like to have paws heavy enough to break a paca's back, how it would feel to lean down to lap with a great pink tongue, to see the reflection of round golden eyes and white whiskers. She wandered. Time ceased to mean anything much.

Maybe it would not be so bad to walk through the forest on four feet. The world would look very different, but things would become very simple. And she would be with Cleis.

She found herself back at the shack, taking a large knife from the table. It did not take long to get back to the ruins. She knelt by the glyph wall. She would cut open her own shoulder and ask Ixbalum to give her the change salve. Then she could join Cleis. They could be together. She laid the knife against the muscle of her left shoulder, and cut. Her blood was shockingly red, the pain incredible.

She blinked at the knife. "What am I doing?"

She had to find a way to get Cleis out, not to lose herself. She threw the knife away from her and stood up, holding her arm. The cut was deep. It needed cleaning up. She had to get back to the shack.

That night, as she lay on her bunk, bandaged shoulder aching, the endless chorus of frogs and insects fell silent. Jane was suddenly full of hope. She pulled on her boots, and went to the door. Then she heard it, a low moaning yowl, like a cat on heat. A big cat. The yowl leapt to a scream, then another. The scream turned into a tight cough. She heard harsh panting, hissing, and then that terrible scream.

"Cleis!" Cats sometimes fought over territory. Jane snatched up the lantern and ran out into the dark, following the noise. Fifty yards into the trees, the screaming stopped, and there was a thrashing in the undergrowth, then silence. Jane ran harder.

There was no sign of the cat, but it had flattened an area of undergrowth with a diameter of about ten feet, and the grass was covered in blood. She cast about for tracks, or a trail of blood, anything. There was nothing. Exhausted, she headed back to the shack and lay down, refusing to imagine what might have happened to Cleis.

Someone was shaking her shoulder. Jane opened her eyes. Cleis stood before her naked, gaunt, holding something. Must be a dream. Cleis was pregnant.

The shaking did not stop.

Gaunt. Jane sat bolt upright. Cleis was holding a baby. "Take her. She can't stay with me." Cleis thrust the child at Jane, then opened the door.

"Wait!"

"I can't. She's been fed. Take her away from here."

"No. I'm not going anywhere without you." Jane climbed out of bed, scrunched the blanket into a nest, and laid the child down. "I'll follow you, leave the baby here."

"You can't."

"I can. I will. You're not well, Cleis. You need to leave with me. I want you to. Please." Cleis stood, uncertain. "Don't you want to?"

"Yes!"

"Then why don't you?"

"I can't!" Cleis backed up against the wall.

Jane sat down. She did not want Cleis to bolt. "Come and sit. Just for a moment. We'll have some tea."

"No. I can't, Jane. I really can't. I have to stay here. Under the trees. It's where I belong now. I need to stay."

"You need to look after your child."

"No. Don't you see? It's stronger even than that. I need to be out there, to live. I need it, like I need water, or air."

"I'll follow you. I'll leave the child here and I'll follow you."

"Then she'll die," Cleis said, sadly. And it was that sadness, that resignation that finally told Jane that Cleis would not change her mind. Could not. That Cleis would rather run through the trees than stay here, or anywhere, with Jane. If it was not for the tiny life on the bed....

"What if she ... what if she grows up to be like you?"

"She won't. If you take her away. She'll never miss what she's never had."

"I love you."

"I know. I'm sorry." She moved to the bed, picked up the baby, put her in Jane's arms. "Love my child for me."

They did not say goodbye.

She wrapped the child carefully in a clean shirt and walked down to the village. Two women took one look at her face and went back inside their huts. Ixbalum's hut was empty. A bunch of children gathered at the edge of the trees. Jane stood in the middle of the clearing and addressed the air. "Where is Ixbalum?"

A chicken clucked.

"Where is Ixbalum?"

A woman put her head out of a hut and called to one of the children, shouting instructions. The girl listened, looked sideways at Jane, then darted into the forest. Jane waited patiently. The baby in her arms yawned and opened its eyes. They were the color of brand new copper pennies.

The girl came back with Ixbalum.

"You did this," Jane said finally. She thought she saw pity on Ixbalum's face, but perhaps she imagined it. "I need your help. I'll need milk." She pointed to her breasts, then the child. Ixbalum walked over to her hut and disappeared inside. Jane waited. She did not know what else to do.

Ixbalum came back out holding a pile of soft rags and a gourd. She held them out. The gourd was full of milk.

Some spilled on Jane's thumb as she took it. She sucked at it: rich, not cow's milk.

"You knew, didn't you? You knew."

But Ixbalum shook her head wearily and pointed to Jane, to the baby, and made a flicking motion with her hand. It was unmistakable: *Go away.*

"I'll go for now, because that's what she wanted. But you better.... You keep her safe for me. Just keep her safe."

The journey to Benque Viejo was not difficult. No more trees had fallen across the skidder trail, and the baby, whom she called Penny, because of her eyes, slept soundly in the cardboard box Jane had strapped into the passenger seat. She stayed in Benque Viejo only long enough to buy diapers and baby formula and a feeding bottle, fill tanks with enough gas to get her to the capital city, Belmopan, and to make a phone call to the niece of the ex-governor, on Ambergris.

"Katherine, I want someone who will fill out a birth certificate, no questions asked."

"Who on earth for?"

"My adopted child."

Silence. "Well, that's a turn up for the books. Are you sure? What will people think if you get back to England with a baby in tow. ..."

"I don't care about that anymore." And she did not. She really did not.

She climbed back in the jeep. Penny opened those startling eyes, stretched. Jane wondered if she would look like Cleis when she was older.

Afterword:
A Word for Human Is Woman

by L. Timmel Duchamp

Nicola Griffith has been making significant contributions to the Grand Conversation of feminist sf for more than a decade now. Across the growing body of her work, it's now possible to discern the development of themes and narrative constructs that engage some of the most interesting threads of the Conversation with fresh and ingenious thinking. Though the richness of "Touching Fire," "Songs of Bullfrogs, Cry of Geese," and "Yaguara" open themselves to a broad spectrum of readings, I would like here to read them together as important contributions to one particular thread of the Conversation.

The Human Condition

Western languages and traditional thought position women in an ambivalent relation to the term *human*. Lou Andreas-Salomé notes this problem in a passage her 1898 novel *Fenitschka*:

> It was strange that he [the character, Werner] found it so difficult to imagine women in their simply human multiplicity and not just on the basis of their sexual nature, not just half-schematically. Whether one idealized them or satanized them, they were always reduced by being isolated in a relation back to the man. Perhaps the so-called sphinxlike character of woman emerged out of woman's full humanness, which was in no way

111

> inferior to man's, out of the fact that this violent simplification could not grasp their humanness.[1]

The inability "to imagine women in their simply human multiplicity" and to grasp "woman's full human-ness" has had far-flung consequences in every area of Western thought and art—and an intimate though often subliminal impact on every girl and woman who engages with art, literature, and the received intellectual tradition. The assertion that the primary work of mimetic literary fiction is to illuminate the human condition is such a com-monplace one that I absorbed this "truth" in secondary school and my first two years of college without question-ing it. The generalization that literature aims to illuminate the human condition implies not only that the very best stories are capable of being understood and appreciated by everyone, but also that they represent the experience of every human, regardless of the particularities of their circumstances (e.g., age, ethnicity, gender, educational and economic status) and historical location. Often a second generalization complements the first: viz., that the "great-er" the work, the more "universal" are its insights.

On the surface, the illumination of the "human condi-tion" would appear to address the experience of everyone, regardless of their differences. The expression "the human condition" assumes that everyone shares the same under-standing of what the essence of "human"—or "man" (the synonym for "human" preferred by traditionalists)—is. And as feminist philosophers have repeatedly observed, the default human is a Caucasian, western, educated male, usually heterosexual.[2] And so a certain amount of imagi-native work has to be done to create the illusion of uni-versality, work that traditional philosophers and scholars so take for granted that they never notice it. To begin with, the default human must (in theory, at least) be stripped of sexuality, immanence, and emotion: pared down, that is, to a core personality located in a mind without a significant body in much the way Descartes prescribed in his influential Method. Most white male philosophers and scholars assume that they achieve such disembodied objectivity in their work, likely because most white men do not perceive themselves as being raced or gendered but only as, simply, "normal": and therefore, simply, human. To undertake this operation of the imagination, one must label all the characteristics that mark the default human as different "inessential" and ignore them. So you're male-gendered? That's inessential; you're heterosexual? inessential (or, if essential, simply "normal"); able-bodied? Caucasian? both inessential.

But in order to adopt the notion of the universality of the default human, those who aren't white, educated males have to perform a second operation of the imagination. People of non-WASP cultures, of different educational backgrounds, of different genders must strip away the characteristics that mark them as different from the default human and then look upon the default human and discover themselves in his image. If they are pregnant women, they must ignore their pregnancy. If they are disabled, they must agree that their disability is inessential to their core personality. If they are of color, they must judge their experiences of racism to form no part of the basic human condition. And so on. Transcending "differences" for most people means taking it for granted that differences don't have anything important to do with who we are and how we live our lives.

Defining The Human

Interestingly, science fiction tends to be less interested in illuminating the human condition than in exploring the meaning and limits of being human. Often when sf explores the meaning and limits of being human it implicitly refuses to take the definition of *human* as a given and questions the very idea that "human nature" is universal across time and space. Mary Shelley's *Frankenstein*—a work of science fiction *avant la lettre*—was one of the first works of fiction to do so. Shelley pits Victor Frankenstein—the perfect embodiment of the default human: male, upper-class, educated—against the creature he has assembled from the parts of corpses and endowed with life.

In a departure from the Gothic sensibility (which many critics see as characterizing *Frankenstein*), Shelley does not portray the creature simplistically as the other (in contrast to Victor's obvious if flawed humanity) and thus as entirely alien to the reader's experience as a human being. Instead, the novel provokes its readers to ask whether this creature, a nameless though sentient assemblage of body parts "not of woman born," is not as human as Victor. Must humanity be regarded as an accidental and fortunate condition of birth bestowed only upon privileged characters like Victor Frankenstein? Or can it also be found in those less favored by fortune? Can humanity be perceived, for instance, in penniless orphans, in slaves, in the misshapen or ugly, in the homeless? What exactly is the definition of *human*?

Exploring the meaning and limits of "man" has always been a major preoccupation of sf. The monstrous, the mutant, the superior freak with abnormal talents or intellect provide sf narratives with the means for examining the definition and limits of human. Stories of the mutant, the monstrous, and the abnormal can result in either expanding the definition of "man" to include those who bear little resemblance to the default human or in rendering differences as signs of an inhuman otherness that ultimately serve as a narrative foil for demonstrating the greater glory of (the default) man.[3] Sf takes no unified ideological position on what is human.

Can A Woman Represent Man?

Until recently, most sf authors preferred to use the words *man* and *mankind* rather than *human* and *humanity.* "Man," in fact, often appears with a single adjective in eponymous sf titles. *The Invisible Man, The Shrinking Man, The Demolished Man, The Illustrated Man, The Omega Man* are only a few examples of many. Even though the man alluded to in the title may be a particular male individual, the use of "man" still performs the routine work of the unmarked term in a binary, where the unmarked term can refer to either the specific (i.e., a male human being) or the general (i.e., the universal human). In other words, "man" in these titles allows both author and reader to unconsciously assume that the eponymous man is in some way representative of the species, however extreme his circumstances and (accidental) individual differences.[4]

Joanna Russ's most famous novel, *The Female Man* (1975), critiques the practice of reading "man" as both marked and unmarked at the same time. Inserting her title into the list above— *The Invisible Man, The Shrinking Man, The Demolished Man, The Female Man, The Illustrated Man, The Omega Man* —creates a telling dissonance, because it draws attention to the fact that the meaning of the titles and the eponymous characters would not be the same were female counterparts substituted for the particular males designated by the titles.[5] Russ's title asks how, if *man* is universal, can the experience of a female character ever represent the human condition? And how can the experiences particular to women be included in the definition and meaning of *human*? As long as a male human serves as the default human, Russ reminds us, the very fact that only a marked term ("woman") can be used to identify the female of the species means that a woman can only be "man" with qualification: viz., a *female* man.[6]

Women writers have long been aware of the problem. I've already mentioned Lou Andreas-Salomé's statement of the problem. Virginia Woolf, Simone de Beauvoir, and many others devoted considerable attention to it. Feminist sf writers, however, have been offering especially astute insight into the problem for decades now, precisely because of sf's interest in exploring the meaning and limits of the human. Katherine Burdekin, who wrote under the pseudonym of Murray Constatine, depicted the problem satirically with her dystopia, *Swastika Night* (1937), in which centuries of degradation have reduced women to the status of breeding cattle.[7] Suzy McKee Charnas raised the question again in her Holdfast Chronicles (1974 and 1978), depicting a harshly male-dominated society that treated women as subhuman in the first novel followed in the second by an all-female society where the *only* humans were women. In Joanna Russ's "When It Changed" (1972), a man newly arrived on Whileaway says to the (human) inhabitants he meets, "Where are all the people?" and the narrator remarks, "I realized then that he did not mean people, he meant *men*, and he was giving the word the meaning it had not had on Whileaway for six centuries." While Charnas and Russ's women characters represent the human when they are situated in societies in which males are absent, the problem returns whenever males enter the story.

Taking another tack, Samuel R. Delany attempts a discursive solution in *Stars in My Pocket Like Grains of Sand* (1984); the unmarked universal pronouns in the world he depicts are female, while the marked, male pronouns are used only to designate an object of desire. Monique Wittig makes rather different discursive moves, attempting to alter "the imaginary formation" so important in creating gender. In a few of her essays in *The Straight Mind* (1992), she claims to eliminate the problem for at least some women by asserting that lesbians are not women. Significantly, *femme*, in Wittig's native tongue, means both "woman" and "wife"; the words "woman" and "women," she observes, are categories describing a social relation, not a biological fact. And in her novel, *Les Guérillères (1969)*, she avoids *femme* and *femmes* as signifiers and uses, instead, *elles*, a pronoun that in *Les Guérillères* serves also as the un-marked collective pronoun that in standard French is *ils*.

Human As Embodied

In her fiction, Nicola Griffith approaches the problem in an entirely new way. First, she creates an exclusively fe-male sexual economy that operates regardless of the pres-ence or absence of males in the narrative, such that only female characters exercise sexual agency or express sexual desire.[8] Among other things, an exclusively female sexual economy precludes women serving to mediate between human and nature and places the narrative focus entirely on the relationships of a set of characters who happen to be female—and are above all representations of the *human*. To use Andreas Salomé's words, it keeps women from being "reduced by being isolated in relation back to the man."

In "Song of Bullfrogs," the opening scene may involve two males, but the story is about Molly and Molly's com-ing to terms with her lover Helen's death. The only sexual images and referents are of women loving. And the nar-rative explicitly represents reproduction as a human—cul-tural—problem. In the story, the meaning of gestation and childbirth is not gendered: the narrative notes that pregnancy and labor are too much for any *human* to sur-vive, since every person alive is physically debilitated.

In "Touching Fire," Kate works in a women's bar. Her world as we see it is determined by women. Nadia has in the past killed a male lover (and thus a male-female sexual relationship is passively admitted into the narrative—a sexual relationship that the male is clearly not "up" to), but again, all narrative agency in the story belongs to women. The male is seen as a passive victim rather than an agent of activity.

"Yaguara" offers an especially clear example of how Griffith's establishment of an exclusively female sexual economy creates an arena of women's actions and desires. Not only are women the only effective actors and decision-makers in the story, but also the narrative's presentation of Cleis's pregnancy renders any male participation in it invisible. The narrative never raises the issue of whose sperm Cleis used and under what circumstances she acquired it. All that matters is that Cleis, desiring to be pregnant and bear a child, achieves her desire. No mention is made of Cleis's father, and the mythological Cleis was, significantly, reputed to be the daughter of Sappho; the narrative hints that Cleis's mother did as Cleis has done.

Although Cleis refers to what it means to be a Latina in the US academy, the issue of sexual oppression is never felt in this or the other stories. By avoiding being caught up in resistance to the status quo, Griffith also avoids taking the status quo as the ground from which she must work, and allows herself to tell alternative—new—stories that would otherwise be impossible to tell. Griffith could have used this gambit to evade sexual politics, but does not. A lesbian sexual economy doesn't make things easy for the characters or suggest that pretending sexual politics away is the solution to sexual oppression. What it does, though, above all, is treat female characters as ordinary humans. That is to say, Griffith's construction of a lesbian sexual economy renders the female sex as unmarked as the male. It asserts that the problems these women characters face are the problems that challenge humans generally, problems that might otherwise be invisible without the benefit of a lesbian sexual economy to illuminate the narrative. Equality with difference insists on an equivalence not based on identity. This can be most sharply seen in "Yaguara," where difference is not sexual difference.

Second, in Griffith's fiction, the problem of defining *human* involves a completely other set of differences than those of gender, such that the contradictions the differences entail demand a complex interrogation along an entire spectrum of positions women (and, by extension, men) can occupy in the world and, therefore, urgent attention to the relationship between human and nature. Since in Griffith's narratives women are not available to mediate the relationship between human and nature (since they figure in Griffith's sexual economy as the default human), when *human* includes female and all that is typically projected onto female (irrationality, messy physicality, emotion, etc), the question about the relation between nature and culture, or between human and nature, becomes a great deal more interesting, and the possible answers to the question much less obvious.

Of all the characters in the stories in this chapbook, Ixbalum integrates nature and culture most successfully—and is in a sense exemplary for what Griffith insists that *human* is (i.e., an amalgamation of nature and culture). As a human, she lives in culture (a culture perhaps not recognized by the capitalist, male-dominated world)—by negotiating her own connection to nature. There is nothing simple about this negotiation, and the narrative takes pains to complicate it by positioning the culture in which Ixbalum lives—i.e., Mayan culture— as opaque to Jane, who at the outset of the story does everything she can to position herself in opposition to nature and in objective control as a conscious producer of European culture. In contrast, Cleis and Nadia are absorbed into nature, although at the beginning of "Yaguara" Cleis lives in the borderlands, being a high-achieving Latina obsessed with reading the glyphs of a non-European culture and language she hopes to bring under the intense, widespread scrutiny of (European) scholarly eyes. Kate is seduced by nature's siren song but is unable to live without culture and cannot see how to negotiate both. And Molly can only distinguish herself from nature, fearful of being eaten up by its lack of history or teleology.

Intimacy (particularly sexual intimacy) seems in these stories to automatically situate characters within nature, such that the intimate relationship is mediated—often troubled by—aspects of culture. To the extent that one human relates sexually to another, she must accept herself as partially belonging to nature. Fear of nature and fear of intimacy go hand in hand; a denial of intimacy is a denial of one's connection to nature. Collectively these stories seem to be arguing that negotiating intimacy (like negotiating one's connection to nature) is an essential aspect of being.[9]

"Human" in Griffith's fiction is above all a being who combines socialization and "crocodile brain"—a being who needs, always, to come to terms with the mix (though usually not doing so successfully). By making female the default gender for human, these stories illustrate how differently "human" must be positioned vis-à-vis nature; they suggest that sf that focuses on the male subject as representative of the human misses crucial aspects of the problem.

Gender, which is a system for making (usually binary hierarchical) meaning, does not exist in these stories. Because of this lack of a functioning system of gender, other expressions of difference become more prominent, and sexual characteristics, desire, and expression are freed of gender-determined connotations. When in "Yaguara" Cleis reveals herself to be pregnant, and later, when Cleis gives birth, we are free to see gestation as essentially human—and when we consider her pregnancy at all, it is with respect to her also being a jaguar and deeply connected to nature—and not a matter of her social and gender positioning.

The narrative sets up a conflict not between nature and culture (in which a woman giving birth is unambiguously relegated to the nature side of the dualism, as the gender system would have it), but as interior to what it means to be human. The human being is born; the human being gives birth. Cleis elects to conceive, elects to give birth—thereby affirming her commitment to the human. The human being must be able to negotiate both culture and nature, which is to say that nature and culture are not assigned according to gendered roles. Cleis's penultimate human (but ungendered) act is giving birth to her child: her pregnancy (and her love for Jane) alone have kept her from becoming wholly animal (i.e., the jaguar that she becomes after she hands her child over to Jane)—which is her true desire. Her choosing to delay becoming fully jaguar brilliantly makes the point that maternity is a part of being human—not exterior to culture and not "animal." Focusing on the gendered character of maternity is what typically renders it nature (animal)— and therefore somehow apart from culture and man (which usually are taken as synonymous with human).

In "Song of Bullfrogs," support from other humans keeps Molly alive—and keeps her part of the human community, even before she chooses to rejoin it. Molly's fall and painful struggle to return to her apartment forces her to understand that she can't "have" nature, and that although she is a part of nature, what distinguishes the human is "intelligence, direction, purpose. And time. Something craneflies did not have." The meaning of gestation and childbirth is not gendered in that story. Gestation and childbirth are, instead, framed as requirements for the species' survival—and thus as an emblem of the human connection with nature. The world of nature—of animals and plants—has no such problem. It is flourishing. Molly's fate is tied up with that of humanity, not nature. It is pointless for Molly even to try to identify herself with nature. Doing so is a dead end.

Interestingly, in "Touching Fire" music is associated with the animal and nature rather than the human and cultural. The story portrays music as a product of Nadia's physical movement. (Whereas in "Yaguara" the product of the human is a child, in "Touching Fire" the product of the non-human is music.) According to Kate, Nadia, who makes this music, "had ripped something away, torn aside the veil we normally wear every day to survive in the city." She does this with her music; she does this when she makes love. Because Kate and Nadia are both women, and men do not figure in the sexual economy of the story, Nadia's being wild and animal-like and Kate's being cultured and human does not amount to a gendered opposition, since the differences between them are not gendered.

Full Humanness

Physiologically speaking, eutherian mammals are default females. "Man" is a species of eutherian mammals (eutherian = placental; mammal = milk-bearing).[10] It is likely that discomfort with this fact might have something to do with the traditional gender-role assignment of "nature" to women and "culture" to men. By insisting that the human must be embodied, and that women negotiate rather than mediate man's relationship to nature, Griffith's stories are not arguing that the correct default for human is female, but that what Andreas-Salomé calls "full humanness" must be included in any depiction of the human condition. Griffith has offered one, immensely successful approach for accomplishing this. Her approach necessarily excludes male sexuality. But then only a few philosophers and writers have yet undertaken to figure fully embodied males as human, much less depict "woman's full humanness."

Endnotes

1 Lou Andreas-Salomé, *Fenitschka*, quoted in Biddy Martin, *Woman and Modernity: The (Life)styles of Lou Andreas-Salomé* (Ithaca. NY: Cornell University Press, 1991), p. 183. The novel was first published in 1898 but according to Martin may have been written as early as 1886.

2 As Monique Wittig notes in "Homo Sum" (1990), "All of us have an abstract idea of what being 'human' means, even if what we mean when we say 'human' is still potential and virtual, has not yet been actualized. For indeed, for all its pretension to being universal, what has been until now considered 'human' in our Western philosophy concerns only a small fringe of people: white men, proprietors of the means of production, along with the philosophers who theorized their point of view as the only and exclusively possible one." Wittig sketches a brief history of the development of binary thinking beginning with Pythagoras.

3 Challenges to the limits of the normative definition of "man" as well as defenses of those limits can be found throughout the history of sf (as well as prior to its history, as in works by not only Shelley, but also H.G. Wells). To cite just a few examples of the numerous authors who have not taken the "human condition" for granted: Olaf Stapledon, Theodore Sturgeon (particularly in *More Than Human*), Samuel R. Delany (particularly in *Stars in My Pocket Like Grains of Sand*), A.E. Van Vogt (in *Slan*), Greg Egan, and Bruce Sterling (in *Schismatrix*).

4 Susan Seidelman's film, *Making Mr. Right*, slyly sends up this conflation of "man" as a particular male with "man" as the quintessence of humanity. In a promotional film within the film, her robotics engineer, Dr. Jeff Peters—who has physically modeled the android Ulysses on himself, complete with a penis of apparently impressive dimensions that can function sexually—says of Ulysses that he "is the closet thing to man," then pauses to tap his own chest for emphasis before finishing his sentence with the word "himself." Later, Peters complains about how most human beings are swimming in emotions, controlled by the chemicals in their medullas. But the android falls in love, and

Peters surreptitiously replaces him on the solo seven-year expedition into deep space for which he had been created. Human nature, in Seidelman's universe, is always embodied, messy, and emotional. Dr. Peters—who points to himself as representing "man"—ends up standing in for the love-sick android. The latter ultimately proves more human than his maker, Dr. Peters, the quintessentially white, educated male who although he identifies himself with the default human in fact represents only an oddity at the limits of human being.

5   Richard Matheson did this with his novel *The Shrinking* Man in the film starring Lily Tomlin as *The Incredible Shrinking Woman* (1981). The re-gendering of the protagonist changes the meaning and tone of the story significantly (not least by rendering it a comedy).

6   Challenging the false universal of male pronouns and male-gendered nouns surely counts as one of the most powerful moves made by second-wave US feminists. Although a few diehards continue to cling to "man" and "he" as applying neutrally to everyone, most people in the US today favor inclusive pronouns and nouns, to the extent that using gender-inclusive language has become almost second-nature for many.

7   Burdekin's sfnal exaggeration of the tendency to regard women as less than fully human is susceptible to being read merely as a critique of Nazi ideology in defense of Western humanist values by those who are oblivious to the problem.

8   I discuss Griffith's female sexual economy at length in my essay "Nicola Griffith's *The Blue Place*," which can be found at http://ltimmel.home.mindspring.com/blue.html.

9   The vision of a character able to negotiate both culture and nature seems, to me, to culminate in Aud, the protagonist of *The Blue Place* and *Stay;* Aud is a hero only to the extent that she can successfully negotiate both culture and nature.

10   For a fascinating discussion of this, see Gwyneth Jones's "Sex: The Brains of Female Hyena Twins" in *Deconstructing the Starships: Science, Fiction and Reality* (Liverpool, 1999).

Nicola Griffith (www.nicolagriffith.com) was born in Yorkshire, England. Her novels (*Ammonite, Slow River, The Blue Place,* and *Stay*) have won several grants and prizes, including the Nebula, Tiptree, and several Lambda awards. She is also the co-editor of the BENDING THE LAND-SCAPE anthology series. She lives with her partner, writer Kelley Eskridge, in Seattle—where she takes enormous delight in everything.

Praise for Nicola Griffith's Fiction

Ammonite

...a self-assured, unselfconscious, convincing depiction of a world without men...doing what only SF can do, and doing it with skill and brio.... It answers the question "When you eliminate one gender, what's left?" ("A whole world," is the answer.)
—Ursula K. Le Guin

Ms. Griffith is an astonishingly gifted writer.... Her work is of the very best in the lesbian and gay literary field.
—Allen Ginsberg

Slow River

Nicola Griffith's elegant, risky science fiction transcends stereotypes about the limitations of that genre.
—Carol Guess

With its persuasive characters trying to form identities in an unstable society, its midnight streets and vast industrial engines, *Slow River* is a powerful prose poem on issues that are already with us.
—*Locus*

The Blue Place

Ultimately...as all good thrillers and all the best literary fiction are, a novel of quests and identity. Griffith's prose is intensely visual, and her sense of place...is beautifully wrought.
Lambda Book Report

Griffith clearly challenges us to understand a radically atypical—or perhaps just typically ignored—aspect of the female psyche: the fine line between brutality and passion.
The Women's Review of Books

Stay

Griffith is a writer of considerable gifts. Her sentences shimmer, her powers of observation and description are razor sharp.
—*The New York Times Book Review*